STAKE YOUR CLAIM

STAKE YOUR CLAIM

•

Kim Watters

AVALON BOOKS
NEW YORK

Library of Congress Catalog Card Number: 2003093921
ISBN 0-8034-9622-2

Published by Thomas Bouregy & Co., Inc.
160 Madison Avenue, New York, NY 10016

PRINTED IN THE UNITED STATES OF AMERICA
ON ACID-FREE PAPER
BY HADDON CRAFTSMEN, BLOOMSBURG, PENNSYLVANIA

To Bill and Shane
Thanks for all your love, support and patience.

To my critique buddies
Carol, Deb, Marion, Sandy & Shelley,
Thanks!

Acknowledgments

A special thanks to:
The late Mason Coggins at the Arizona Mining and Mineral Museum, for his time, knowledge and experience;

All the folks at the Asarco Mine in Sahuarita, Arizona, for their insight, expertise and an exceptional tour; and

Jack Thompson, for sharing his knowledge of airplanes.

Any errors contained within are the sole responsibility of the author.

Prologue

"Today's the day. Today's the day," Eden Delgado chanted, skipping toward the mine. In one hand she carried her daddy's lunch pail. In the other, her daddy's old miner's hat.

As she skipped by the front of the maintenance shop, she paused to wave to the old man who stood next to a yellow truck wiping his hands on a rag. "Hello, Mr. Brewster. Did you know I'm eight today?"

The bald man quit whistling and returned her wave. "Hello to you too, Eden. Of course I did." Grinning, he tucked the rag into the back pocket of his coveralls and motioned to her. "Now, come here and get your hug."

Eden hopped over to the wide door and stopped—close enough to smell the diesel fumes and grease, but far enough away so she wouldn't get in trouble by the mine's owner, Mr. Kipling. She wasn't allowed in there because of some kind of ocean rules. Though she couldn't figure out why—the ocean was miles and miles away. Soon, Daddy had promised her, he'd take her and her brother, Adam, to see the ocean; then she could figure it out herself.

"I hear your daddy's got something really special planned for you," Mr. Brewster continued. "Come to think of it, the missus and I got something for you too. Happy birthday, honey." He produced a piece of candy from behind her ear, one of Eden's favorite tricks. She giggled.

Placing the hat and lunch box on the ground, Eden accepted the cherry gumdrop, unwrapped it, and plopped it in her mouth. "Mmmm—my favorite. Thank you, Mr. Brewster. This is going to be my best birthday ever."

"Hurry on now, don't keep your daddy waiting."

"Bye. See you tomorrow." Eden hugged her Grandpa Fred's friend, picked up her things, and ran to the entrance.

Suddenly, the earth shook beneath her feet. A flash of light spewed forth from the opening in the mountain, followed by a blast of hot air. Thrown off balance, Eden fell. As she sat there dazed, choking on dirt, she heard only the deafening roar of falling rock.

Then—silence.

"Daddy?"

Standing on shaky legs, she stumbled toward the entrance. Her ears still rang from the loud noise. A layer of dust blinded her. She struggled forward, stubbing her toes on large stones and tripping over smaller ones. Instead of an opening, she bumped headfirst into rock.

Pain shot through her forehead as she fell backwards. She placed a hand over the spot to stop the ache. It didn't help. Beneath her palm, it felt wet.

Eden needed to find Daddy. He'd know what to do.

As she crawled to her feet she licked her lips, tasting dirt and blood. Everything was going wrong. Her head hurt. The lift was late. Where was Daddy?

The off-pitch wail of a siren sounded, scaring her. Daddy hadn't said anything about an emergency drill today.

Upset, she held out her hands and searched for the entrance again. She felt only a wall of stone. Confused, she staggered left. Then right. Her palms and fingers scraped against the rough surface. There was no opening.

"It's gone. Where did it go?" She coughed. The dust bothered her throat and burned her eyes. She balled her fists and wiped away the tears and blood, then shook her head, bewildered at the huge rock in front of her. "The entrance should be right here."

The siren screamed in her ears, joined by shouts and the sound of footsteps. Her skin prickled, her stomach churned, her head hurt. Something was really, really wrong.

"Daddy?" she shrieked, clawing at the boulder. "Daddy, where are you?"

Chapter One

Twenty years later . . .

"Just what kind of joke *is* this?" Eden Delgado questioned, placing her hands on her hips as she read the notice posted on the community bulletin board outside the Prosperity post office. "How can there be an open house at the Kipling mansion? That place has been abandoned for years. Ever since . . ." She fell silent, unable to force out the words caught in her throat.

Around her, sounds of the small Arizona community intensified: a barking dog, kids laughing, the swoosh of the post office door. She glanced up and down the four-lane street that ran through the center of town. Everything seemed normal—except for the blue signs posted everywhere.

Her attention shifted back to the sign in front of her. Using her index finger as a guide to make sure she didn't skip a word, Eden read the entire notice out loud. " 'Open house at the Kipling mansion this Saturday at seven o'clock. Food and drink provided. Everyone welcome to attend and discuss the future of Prosperity. Signed, J. A. Kipling.' "

In disbelief, Eden read the notice five more times. "Discuss the future? What's that supposed to mean? The Kiplings have no business—" Comprehension set in. "The mine. They want to reopen the mine."

So the rumors of activity at the mansion had been true. She went numb and turned to lean against the brick building for support. The solid wall offered no comfort. Sucking in a ragged breath of warm summer air, she closed her eyes to block out the image of the sign, but the words were burned into her brain. This could not be happening.

"Daddy!" The sob spilled from her lips. Even after all this time, it still hurt. Her father's death had left a huge void in her life that nothing could fill.

Abuelo had tried, but it just wasn't the same. She loved her grandfather, but it should've been her father who took her to the emergency room when she fell out of the tree and broke her arm, her father who taught her to drive when she was sixteen, her father who sat there proudly when she graduated from high school.

But no, the Kiplings had taken that all away from her.

Jagged pain sliced through the numbness. Eden's carefully held emotions slipped and her temper flared. "How dare they reopen the mine!"

Twenty years still wasn't enough time to mend all the wounds inflicted on her or the citizens of Prosperity. Not only had they closed the mine after pulling her father and the others out, the Kiplings had disappeared from sight, leaving the town close to financial ruin and the miners' families scrambling to bury the dead and make ends meet. To this day, Prosperity had never really recovered.

Dragging her gaze down to the cracked, sagging sidewalk, Eden noticed a weed struggling to grow where some concrete had fallen away. The much-needed repairs had never been done, nor the road repaved, as promised.

Shattered dreams and broken promises. That was what the name Kipling symbolized.

Intense bitterness welled inside her, mingling with her anger. Charles Kipling had allowed seventeen men to die in that cave-in; her father one of them. How many more lives would the Kiplings put in danger if they reopened the mine?

She would *not* allow anyone else to suffer because of the Kiplings. Sure, the town needed money, but the mine was not the answer. She'd find another way.

Eden whirled around and yanked the sign off the

board. "Discuss the future, J. A. Kipling? I don't think so." She tore it to shreds, much to the delight of the three old men sitting on the bench on the other side of the door.

"Give that no-good Kipling grandson heck, Eden." A Larson brother cackled, his laughter giving her courage. The other one thumped his metal cane in approval while the third gave her a thumbs-up.

"You're darned right I will. The Kiplings will be sorry they ever stepped foot in this town again!" Forgetting to collect her mail, she marched away from the bulletin board, tore down the signs attached to the post office doors, then headed across the street toward the next blue slip of paper tacked to the pole out in front of the Dry Gulch Restaurant & Bar.

A pick-up game of baseball in the middle of Main Street caught her attention just long enough to dodge an errant ball. "Brandon Garrett, how many times do I have to tell you to take your game to the park before you hurt someone?" she yelled as a pimply-faced boy ran past her.

"Sorry, Miss Eden," he called back, grinning sheepishly.

"Well, don't let it happen again, or I'll tell your Uncle Tyler."

She ignored the rest of the boys as she walked over to the post and grabbed another sign. "Take that, J. A. Kipling." Eden ripped the paper in half, enjoying the sound. "And that. And that." She dumped the pieces into the black old-fashioned wastebasket outside the bar.

"Hey, stop that!" a voice protested.

Eden paid no attention. Her father and his memories were more important than the blue piece of paper. She would not allow this J. A. Kipling, or anyone for that matter, to breeze back in to town and reopen the mine. Too many people had already suffered. A mixture of determination, pride, and anger propelled her as she continued down the street, tearing down the signs as she went.

"I said stop." The voice had grown closer now, but driven by her anger, Eden kept going. As she reached out to pull down another notice outside the Wells Fargo Bank & Company, a hand, fingers splayed, smacked against the paper. A man's hand, if she could go by the long, tanned fingers and the harsh voice that accompanied it. "Don't."

"Don't what?" Eden retorted. "Don't remove these illegally posted signs? I don't think so. Now, if you'll excuse me—" Lifting her chin, she turned and attempted to navigate around him.

"Not so fast." He raised his other arm, effectively barring her path. "Why are you tearing down my sign?"

Her body went cold, her spine rigid. He had to be one of them. One of the despised. One of the Kiplings. J. A. Kipling, to be exact. Who else would object to her actions?

Eden returned the angry man's glare—and almost swallowed her tongue. Lord, he was big . . . and tall. Taller than her friend Tyler, and Tyler was the tallest man in town. Her mouth went dry. Not only did his size intimidate her, he was young, close to her own age, and he looked nothing like the Charles Kipling she remembered.

Eden forced air into her lungs as she tilted her head back to look into the most incredible eyes she'd ever seen. They were as blue as the sapphires in her collector's book of precious stones. Shaken, her gaze traveled down, past his perfectly formed nose, past what she considered two very kissable lips, and focused on the blond, curly hair protruding from the vee of his blue polo shirt.

He was the best-looking man she'd ever laid eyes on. She shuddered involuntarily. Too bad he was the grandson of a murderer. Her father had died for this man's family and she would *not* be attracted to him. Even if he was the proverbial 'last man on earth'. No matter how much this Kipling made her heart flutter, her family name and her father's memories deserved better.

"Well, I'm waiting," the man growled impatiently. "Answer me."

At his demand, Eden snapped. Forget hospitality, forget composure. He sure had the nerve—the gall—to traipse back in to town and attempt to continue where his grandfather left off. She would *not* be treated this way. Prosperity was her town, not his, no matter *who* he was. “No. Now let me pass.”

“Fine.” His quiet tone broke the uneasy silence that stretched between them. “I’d like to know your reasons, but I’ll settle for your word. Promise me you’ll quit tearing down my signs and I’ll let you go. It’s your choice.”

“My choice? I actually have one? And if I refuse? What will you do then, Mr. Kipling? Throw me over your shoulder and carry me off like some . . . some Neanderthal?”

“Now, that’s a thought.” He folded his arms across his chest and stared at her, the fire in his eyes and the twitching muscle at his jaw emphasizing his words.

Eden took in his broad shoulders and muscular arms. Her mouth felt like someone had stuffed a bunch of cotton balls in it. He probably wouldn’t hesitate to do whatever he wanted. The Kiplings never did. Her family and the town had paid the ultimate price.

Her indignation rose at the thought of herself slung over his shoulder as he carried her through town like a sack of potatoes. He wouldn’t. Not with a Delgado! Tossing her braid behind her shoulder, she spoke with as much dignity as she could muster. “You wouldn’t, would you?”

“Don’t push your luck,” Jake Kipling grumbled under his breath. He knew he’d get some opposition about reopening the mine from the townspeople at the open house or the town council meeting tomorrow night. But he figured it would be from the men, and the old-timers, not this half-pint female standing in front of him.

Rubbing his knuckles against the day-old growth on his chin, he contemplated his next course of action. Letting her go would be the wisest thing, but Jake usually didn't adhere to society's rules. If he had, he'd be a lawyer, not a mining engineer. His grandfather, Charles Kipling, hadn't spoken to him for almost four years after he'd made that decision. At the time, Jake hadn't understood his grandfather's behavior. Not that it would have made any difference. Had Jake known, his desire would have been that much stronger.

"Excuse me?" The question brought his attention back to the woman in front of him.

"I said, don't push your luck. Now are you going to answer my question, or not?" As he stepped back, he tugged at his earlobe and openly stared at her. A thick, dark mahogany braid caressed her neck, while wispy bangs framed her oval face. But it was her eyes that captured his attention. They were rich brown, like the dark chocolate milk his nanny used to make for him at bedtime. A funny sensation churned in his stomach, but he ignored it.

He didn't need another complication right now. Especially one with a huge chip on her shoulder.

"I should think it's quite obvious, Mr. Kipling. Neither I, nor the town, want you here."

"Is that so?" Jake said more to himself than the

woman in front of him. His appraisal of the town was that it was in a state of disrepair, almost borderline neglect. The revenue the mine would produce would no doubt cover the costs of renovations for the downtown district, plus provide jobs for at least fifty people, if not more.

It was his duty as a Kipling, his mother had pointed out, to make sure that happened. It was also his chance to become his own boss and connect with part of his past. And nothing—not even this woman who so openly opposed him and attracted him—was going to stand in his way.

"Yes, it is so. We don't want you here. Now if you don't mind . . ."

"But I do mind." He allowed her to pass, but fell in step beside her. They'd only walked a few yards when she whirled around to face him.

"Maybe I haven't made myself clear, Mr. Kipling." She placed her hands on her hips and tilted her head to look up at him. "I don't want you here. The town doesn't want you here. In fact, the whole state of Arizona doesn't want you here. Is that clear?"

"Perfectly," Jake replied, his expression hardened, his voice like steel. "But I don't intend to listen to you." *I don't listen to anybody anymore, except myself, or the town council's decision.*

The woman's reaction was priceless. Her mouth dropped open, and her eyes grew as big as saucers.

But Jake made a big mistake in letting his gaze wander.

"Look, Miss." He glanced away. "This is getting old. I just want you to stop tearing down my signs. Is *that* clear?"

He wanted more than anything to keep up the banter, except it was hot—and humid. Even in the higher elevations in Southeastern Arizona, summer was definitely hotter than upstate New York. Jake mopped his brow with his sleeve.

"Perfectly." Eden reached over him and grabbed the sign posted behind his head and tore it up. If he thought his presence would deter her, he'd have to think again. Because if he wouldn't quit, neither would she.

"Come on." He clamped a hand around her arm, and propelled her into the street.

"Where we going?" She pulled against his hold, but Jake didn't release her.

"Obviously we need to discuss this further, but I'm not going to do it out here. We're going to get a soda."

"But the bar is the other direction." She stopped herself in mid-stride just long enough to glance around to see who else had witnessed this public humiliation.

Two of her grandfather's cronies sat on the bench under the dark green awning outside Ybarra's Barbershop shaking their heads in disbelief. Barbara Fulton, the town gossip, stood by the front door of Whitey's

Grocery Store talking to the pastor's wife. *Great!* Eden prayed she'd be back at the diner in time to tell her side of the story.

"We're not going to the bar."

Eden still tried to be civil even though her father would turn over in his grave if he saw her hobnobbing with the enemy. "Then where are we going?"

"Somewhere a little more private."

"I don't think so." She dug in the heels of her hiking boots into the street and forced them to stop.

For a second.

The next thing she knew, Kipling wrapped an arm around her waist and pulled her back. An errant fly ball bounced past them, hitting the ground with a thud. As it now rolled harmlessly down the street, Eden squirmed, but he didn't release his hold. "I think it's safe now. You can let go of me anytime you like, Mr. Kipling."

"Fine." He helped her to the sidewalk, then freed her.

With her knees still quivering like a bowl of Abuelo's infamous lime Jell-O, she sank down on a wrought-iron bench. The air rushed from her lungs as the warm metal hit her square across the shoulder blades.

"Are you okay?"

That was a loaded question. "Yes." She was okay physically, but emotionally was another story. He'd saved her from serious injury. That ball had hit the street hard enough to create a cloud of dust. It probably would have knocked her unconscious, or worse. And he had saved her.

Now she was indebted to a man she despised.

Brandon Garrett ran by, mumbling what Eden took as another apology, before he scooped up the ball.

"Your uncle will definitely hear about this," she called after him breathlessly. Except he was no longer in sight. He and the other boys had scattered.

"Those kids ought to know better than to play in the street," Kipling said. "Why don't they go to the park?"

"Maybe because the park is in such bad shape." Eden concentrated on her breathing. In, out. In, out. Once she regained a normal pattern, she'd work on her heart rate. Its frantic beat was from her close call, nothing more.

"Too bad. Those kids will have to find somewhere else to play until the park can be fixed. Now about that soda—"

"Look, it's really not necessary. I can . . ." Her words died in her throat as she glanced up at the man who'd held her captive. His gaze brought color to her cheeks that had nothing to do with the unseasonably warm weather.

"I insist. We Kiplings have always prided ourselves on our manners. And I think we still have some things to discuss."

Taking her firmly but gently by the elbow again, he

helped her up and escorted her to the old surveyor's office. Once inside, he shut the door with his foot, settled her into a well-worn leather chair, then opened the door to the small refrigerator next to the desk.

"Regular or diet?"

"Just because I'm a woman doesn't mean I don't like things with sugar. In fact, the more sugar, the better."

"I'll have to remember that. Regular it is then." Flipping the tab open, he handed the soda to her.

She drank, allowing the cool liquid to soothe her parched throat. "I'd prefer you didn't. Thank you."

"Now why are *you* opposed to my being here?"

She inhaled, taking in the stale, musty air in the room. His presence was doing crazy things to her, and this time she couldn't blame it on exertion.

"I'm surprised you have to ask. You should know. Or don't you know the history of this town?"

Jake backed away, not taking his gaze off her as he leaned against the old desk. "I know too well what happened."

"If you know, then why are you here?"

Jake smothered a smile. Just this morning, when the hot water heater went out again at the mansion, he'd asked himself the same question. But he'd never forget the answer, just like he'd never forget the promise he'd made to his mother.

"I have eyes," he said, trying to reason with her.

"And it doesn't take a genius to figure out this town needs jobs, the buildings repaired. I want to—"

"We can do it ourselves, given enough time," she countered. "We don't need you or your mine to do that."

"Don't you?"

"You know nothing about us or our circumstances, and—"

"I know more than you think I do."

Anger lit up her eyes again. "Do you?"

Jake bit back his retort. As she crossed her arms in front of her, he noticed some pretty tantalizing curves. He didn't like petite, shapely brunettes; he liked tall, leggy blondes. Blondes who were sophisticated and demure, blondes who didn't question his authority, blondes with no emotional baggage.

Yet, when he held her a few minutes before, Jake had to struggle to remember this woman wanted no part of his dreams. She'd made that perfectly clear. Starting up with the opposition wasn't going to solve the problem.

Well, that depended on which problem he thought about. His current problem, yes; the real problem, no. But he also knew, as a Kipling, that it wasn't a gentlemanly thing to do. Disgusted with himself, Jake shook his head.

Hadn't he learned enough from his mother's mistakes?

"Yes. Miss—" Jake hadn't seen any ring, but these

days you could never tell. He didn't need some territorial male coming after him; he already had enough problems.

"What is your name anyway?" For some reason he couldn't fathom, he had to find out. From her, not a third party on the street. "You don't have to tell me, but in a town this size, it shouldn't be too hard to find out."

"You're right." She approached him and placed her hands, palms flat, on the desk. "I don't have to tell you, but I will. My name is Eden."

"Eden?" He blinked at the name. "That's unusual. Eden what?"

She squared her shoulders and looked him straight in the eye. "Eden Marie Consuela Delgado."

"Eden Marie Consuela Delgado," he repeated, his hand dropping to rest on the desk. Jake could see the Hispanic influence now in her coloring, her pale olive complexion kissed lightly by the sun. Still, her heritage didn't concern him at the moment, her name did.

"Delgado." Drumming his fingers against the wood, Jake searched his memory. He drew a blank. The long days and even longer nights were finally taking their toll on him. "Why does that sound so familiar?"

She raised her eyebrows. "I'm shocked. I thought you knew the history of this town. If you did—"

"Delgado. Miguel Delgado." The name sprung from his lips as he remembered the list his mother had saved for him, the list that named the men killed at the mine.

"My father." Her bitter expression was not lost on him. "Now do you understand, Mr. Kipling?"

"Yes." Jake understood too well. A heaviness settled on him that he didn't want to dwell on; he didn't have the time, or the energy. "And please don't call me Mr. Kipling, it reminds me of my grandfather. My name is Jonathan Alexander. My friends call me Jake." Rising to his full six-foot-five height, he offered her his hand.

Eden blatantly ignored his outstretched palm as she turned and strode to the door. She paused at the threshold and looked back at him. "Thanks again for the soda, Mr. Kipling. Just remember, I'm not one of your friends. Nor will I let you reopen the mine. I'll fight you on this with every last ounce of energy I possess."

Chapter Two

"Eden Delgado, what on earth possessed you to do such a thing?" Mrs. Jackson chastised as she wiped down the counter after the last of the lunch crowd left Delgado's Diner. "What would your dear father, God rest his soul, think of your actions today?" The matronly woman made the sign of the cross over her ample bosom.

At the mention of her father, Eden pulled out the comfortably worn barstool and laid her forehead on the cracked, silver-speckled white Formica.

"I don't know, Nana. I'd hope he'd be proud of me."

But would he? Eden knew destroying another man's property was wrong. Yet when she'd seen those signs, anger overruled her upbringing, and she couldn't stop herself.

Eden heard the soft plop of the rag dropping to the counter before Mrs. Jackson heaved herself onto another stool and dragged her into her arms. Since her mother's death a year after her father's, Mrs. Jackson, whom Eden affectionately called Nana, had stepped in to help Abuelo raise her and her brother, Adam.

"Oh, honey." Mrs. Jackson's gentle voice enveloped her as it had many times in the past. "Your daddy was always so proud of you, your mama too."

Sighing, Eden lifted her head from the counter and rested it on Mrs. Jackson's shoulder. Jake Kipling's presence had sent her world spinning off its axis, and she thought about how her parents had been killed by the Kipling family—her father in the mine, her mother from a broken heart.

"How can they do this to us? Haven't we suffered enough?"

She heard Mrs. Jackson count to ten under her breath before the woman replied, "Maybe reopening the mine might not be a bad thing, honey."

"How can you say that, Nana?" Eden sat up in surprise. "Your husband was also one of the miners killed." Maybe the rumors that Mrs. Jackson was a bit addled were true. Eden herself had noticed some peculiarities over the past few months but had dismissed them, figuring it was age-related.

Mrs. Jackson didn't answer right away and Eden noticed her attention had strayed to Abuelo, who stood behind the opening in the wall where the food orders came up, his back to them as he cleaned the grill. The scraping sound clashed with the mariachi music in the background.

"Twenty years is a long time, Eden. Life goes on, whether we want it to or not. My Nate wouldn't want me to dwell on the past anymore than your daddy, honey. Now let's get this place cleaned up before your grandfather accuses us of cackling like old hens again." Mrs. Jackson patted a stray strand of white hair back into place before standing.

"Okay." The odor of frying oil lingered in the air, comforting Eden. She'd grown up here, immersed in this business since she'd been able to walk. With all the things happening around her, at least Abuelo remained a constant.

Feeling better, she grabbed a tray along with the jugs filled with salt and pepper and headed toward the tables by the window. Mondays and Wednesdays were her afternoons off, but she didn't mind helping. She had nothing else to do.

She sat down on the patched maroon vinyl bench, snatched the shakers, and removed the lids. "Jonathan Alexander Kipling. What kind of name is that?" she muttered as she scooped salt from the jug with a well-used Styrofoam cup and poured it into the little glass bottle. "A horrible one, if you ask me. No wonder he prefers Jake!"

A shadow crossed in front of the window. Eden glanced up to see her nemesis pause between the white painted letters 'D' and 'e' of Delgado's Diner and look at her before walking away. She swallowed, her task forgotten until the salt granules poured over the top and onto her hand.

"Jesus, Mary and Joseph," Mrs. Jackson gasped. Eden turned in time to see a bottle fall from the older woman's grasp. Glass and ketchup flew everywhere. "Who was that?" she choked, her complexion paling as she gripped the ledge.

Eden leaped from her seat. Shuttling around the counter, she lunged for one arm as Abuelo caught the other. Together, they pulled Mrs. Jackson to the nearest chair and sat her down before she passed out completely.

"*Nieta*, get Wilma a glass of water," Abuelo ordered.

"Who was that?" Mrs. Jackson questioned again faintly. Eden noticed that some of the color had returned to her face as she set down the iced water.

"*That* was Jonathan Alexander Kipling himself, Nana," she announced. "The man who's come to save the town."

"My goodness, for a moment I thought it was my Nate."

"That's impossible, Wilma, and you know it. Have you been taking your medication?"

Eden saw Abuelo roll his eyes as he touched a finger to his brow, confirming that the talk around town was true.

"Folks, please." Mayor Paul Clifford raised his voice to be heard over the squabbles breaking out in the gym. Eden saw him reach for his gavel in order to regain control. The loud bang silenced the room and brought everyone's attention back to the makeshift dais where the town council sat. "Thank you. I realize this is a sensitive subject, yet an important one for the future of our community."

The portly mayor paused for a moment and looked directly at Eden. She lifted her head and returned his stare. *She* wasn't going to back down. Mayor Clifford pulled a handkerchief from his jeans and mopped his balding head before transferring his gaze to Jonathan Alexander Kipling, seated on the other side of the aisle.

Behind the mayor, Eden noticed the four other town council members shift in their seats while Greta Reinhart, the librarian, fidgeted with her eyeglass chain. They'd had to move the meeting from the town hall to the Prosperity grade school at the last minute to accommodate the large number of people in attendance. She'd lost count, but figured there had to be at least three hundred people.

Eden leaned back in her folding chair, satisfied. With the exception of the Brabants, every person who had lost a family member in the cave-in was present.

"As you know," the mayor continued, "Mr. Kipling has asked the town to reopen Cholla Way, which all of you know provides access to Mina de Cobre. If we grant his request, Mr. Kipling has agreed to improve the road at his own expense. He's also agreed to answer any questions and address your concerns for opening the mine."

Arguments broke out around the room, until the mayor silenced them again with the gavel. Eden's friend, Tyler McAllen, a county deputy sheriff, walked to the front and stood off to the side of the dais, leaving two other deputies standing near the exits.

Even as part of the opposition, Eden prayed the meeting didn't come to blows. Violence, outside of tearing up a few sheets of paper, never settled anything.

"To make the discussions go quicker," Mayor Clifford said as he shook off his sport jacket and tossed it onto his chair, "the council has decided to forgo the use of the podium. Anyone who wishes to speak will stand and do so from their seat. I will moderate. I now turn the floor over to Mr. Kipling to start the proceedings."

Unlike his grandfather, Jake hated public speaking. He had ever since Mrs. Longley's fourth grade class and her incessant demands for oral reports.

But Jake stood anyway, wishing he'd worn a polo shirt. In his decision to make a good impression, he'd donned a suit and tie. Mistake. One look at the assembled crowd and he knew he'd overdressed for the occasion. Blue jeans and T-shirts were the norm. Not even the mayor sported a tie.

Beads of perspiration gathered on his forehead, and sweat formed under his arms and beneath his collar. He longed to loosen the paisley stranglehold, but after one look at Eden, sitting so demurely in her peach-colored sundress, nixed the idea.

The challenge written on her face renewed his determination. Jake was not going to let her, or anyone else, keep him from proving his worth as a man and as a Kipling. Especially since he knew that reopening the mine was in the best interests of everyone sitting in the room—Eden included. He had to convince them tonight, or at the open house on Saturday.

Clearing his throat, he turned and angled himself so he could address the council and most of the townspeople at the same time. "First of all, on behalf of my family, I'd like to extend my sincerest apologies to the families of the seventeen workers who lost their lives in the unfortunate accident twenty years ago. I know that I cannot replace what has been lost to you. But—"

"Then what are you here for, Yankee?"

Raucous laughter from the back row filled the room. Several other people joined in—even a member from the council. This wasn't going well, and he hadn't even started. Jake made eye contact with the perpetrator, a wizened old man in overalls. To his surprise, the old-timer looked away first, to the disapproval of his compatriots. They booed and hissed and shoved each other until the two sheriff's deputies stationed by the back door approached them.

The other deputy in front paced to the dais, grabbed the gavel from the mayor, and banged it on the podium. "Settle down, people," he bellowed. "Let the man speak. Anyone who steps out of line again will spend the night in lockup." Jake watched as the tall blond man surveyed the room before coming to rest on the woman in the peach dress. "That goes for you too, Eden."

Her ghost of a smile didn't reassure Jake. Nor did the sounds of rustling papers or hushed voices over the squeaking of metal chairs from the town's restless citizens.

"Please continue, Mr. Kipling. I don't think there will be any more trouble," the deputy announced and moved back to his position by the wall.

Jake acknowledged him with a slight nod. At least the law was on his side. Now he needed to convince the town. "How many of you would like a new car? A new television? A new air conditioner?" Everyone in the room remained motionless. "Go ahead. It's okay to raise your hands." One by one, people began raising their hands until every hand was lifted except Eden's.

"Copper is the answer, folks. Every item I listed, as

well as many other appliances that make our lives easier, is made with copper. In fact, an average single family home uses roughly four hundred and thirty-nine pounds of copper. Add it up, folks." He warmed to his topic. "Consumption has risen the last ten years. So has demand. Prices are good and new mines are slated to be opened in the coming years to meet this demand. If the counsel approves the reopening of Cholla Way, Mina de Cobre can be one of them."

"That's good for you, what about us?"

"Yeah, what about us?" Several other people chimed in.

"Once we bring in the equipment, conduct our surveys, and re-establish the ore base, reopening the Kipling mine would provide new tax revenues, jobs, and—"

"What kind of jobs?" a young man, barely in his early twenties, questioned. Beside him, a woman Jake guessed to be his wife held a fidgety infant.

"How many men will it take? When will it start?" another chorus of voices wanted to know.

"How do we know he won't hire outsiders and bring 'em in? They done it before," a man shouted from the center of the room. Around him, Jake noticed several people nodding their heads in agreement.

"I know several of you lost positions when the Hattersfield Mine closed last winter. I promise to hire as many qualified people from Prosperity as possible," he stated, practically shouting over the din in the room.

"Well, I don't believe him," an old woman screeched as she stood. "The Kiplings have always broken their promises. Both to the living and the dead." With that, she left, hobbling off with the help of a walker.

This definitely wasn't going well. Another drop of sweat trickled from his hairline, down his cheek and continued to hug the contours of his face until it disappeared under his collar. He longed to re-adjust the scratchy material, but to do so would show weakness.

He squared his shoulders. 'A Kipling doesn't give up.' Charles's authoritative voice pounded into his brain like a cane striking a hardwood floor. His spine straightened automatically at the memory of the ivory staff that accompanied the old man everywhere—and how he'd used it. Jake destroyed those thoughts like he'd destroyed the cane after his death. Neither had a place in his life.

Jake couldn't deny he was a Kipling, nor did he want to. The name opened doors and afforded him privileges. But he was only half of one. His father's heritage ran through his veins too—the blood of a common laborer.

Jake had never met his father, but his mother had left him a few trinkets and letters. And it was her dying wish that he come to Prosperity because his father would have wanted him to continue the mining operations.

He disregarded the rest of his prepared speech. In

such a hostile environment, most of the people wouldn't listen anyway, and since this was the West they'd probably already strung up a rope, but he had to finish.

"In conclusion, I'd like to thank you all for attending tonight. I'll be happy to answer any further questions you may have regarding this issue, now or any time in the future. To Miss Delgado," Jake acknowledged her with a nod, "and the rest of the families who lost loved ones, again, I'm very sorry for all the pain and suffering my family has caused you. While I cannot replace your loved ones, I do want to try and give this community something in the way of a better life, better jobs, and a safer work environment."

He paused for dramatic effect, making eye contact with several people before resting his gaze on Eden. "Based on some of my grandfather's notes and the land structure, I believe that the mine will produce a million dollars a year in net revenue, possibly more. Think about what that would mean in the way of jobs, tax revenues, and the economy for Prosperity. All I ask of you is to reopen the road to the mine. I promise you, you won't be sorry."

Jake could have heard a pin drop as he took his seat.

The semblance of control Eden had mustered since yesterday sputtered. She was glad her jaw was attached to her skull or it would have dropped to the floor. The nerve of the man to apologize not once, but twice, for the accident. His attitude shrugged off the lives of the miners, making them as inconsequential as the ticks she pulled off the family dog every so often. Her father and the others were nothing but a statistic to be shoved aside as an inconvenience for the almighty dollar.

She could not allow that to happen. Eden had promised herself years ago to keep the good memories of those seventeen men alive. Allowing the mine to open would defile all she'd worked so hard to achieve. Her father deserved more, and so did each and every miner killed.

Her hands were clamped so tightly together her knuckles turned white. She forced herself to remain in the hard metal folding chair. If not, she'd strangle him with that expensive piece of silk around his neck.

Whispers turned to a loud buzz as comprehension sank in. The noise grated on her nerves until Tyler McAllen stepped up to the dais again, shouting, "That's enough, people. One at a time."

Eden looked at the council and wondered if the mayor, from the expression on his face, had swallowed his tongue. Then glancing around, she saw the shock register on the faces of her friends and neighbors. The ensuing silence shattered what little control she'd retained. Even the paper fans had quit rustling, forgotten in the hands of the stunned citizens. Only the din of the air conditioning unit working overtime echoed through the massive room.

No one had any more questions? They were all going to believe this—this Kipling? Eden fought the urge to scream by biting her lip. This was not happening.

"How do we know he's telling the truth?" Her neighbor shuffled to his feet, casting his eyes around the room until they came in contact with hers. Eden wanted to run and throw her arms around the tiny man, glad someone else had the courage to speak.

"How do we know he's not?"

The discord mounted again as families and neighbors gathered to press the issue. As the din swelled to an uproar, Eden heard Mayor Clifford bang the gavel on the podium. Goosebumps rose on her arms from the energy coursing through the room. Her side was winning. How could the council approve something so controversial? She almost tasted the heady sweetness of victory.

Eden turned to stare triumphantly at Jake and was startled to find his eyes already fixed on her. She quit breathing. Her mind went blank and her confidence tumbled to her toes along with her already rapidly beating heart.

She held his gaze even after a man jumped up beside Jake and pulled off his own battered baseball cap, holding it uneasily between his dirt-stained fingers. "We all know this town could use the jobs since the Hattersfield Mine and the glass factory closed in Carter."

A crescendo of voices agreed in the back of the gym.

"But how long will it stay open?"

"Where do I sign up?"

"Will families who lost relatives get preferential treatment?"

More shouts from the corner brought Eden's attention around. She detected the energy shift in the room. Volatile and dangerous. Yet not as dangerous as the man sitting ten feet away.

A smattering of applause interspersed with more boos and hisses rang in her ears as she fixed her stare on the restless crowd, only too aware of Jake's gaze on her. The blood pounding through her veins almost drowned out the rest of the proceedings.

"How do we know he's really a Kipling?"

"Sit down, Frank." Mayor Clifford shooed him off. "You've been drinking again." Some of the old-timers guffawed as the old man stumbled from the room.

Suddenly, an image of her father's face flashed through her consciousness. Like a picture without sound, she could see him clearly, his lips forming words that she strained to hear. The only sound she recognized was her own sob.

Sprung like an over-tightened rubber band, Eden shot to her feet. This had to stop. Now. Mentally anchoring her feet to the floor to keep from pacing, she faced the council and forced her hands to remain at her sides.

"Let's not forget what happened twenty years ago," she began, gathering her courage when she saw the sympathetic looks. "We don't need the mine to save Prosperity, we have the power to do it ourselves. In a couple of years, with a little hard work, we can follow in the footsteps of Bisbee and Jerome, and other mining towns who have bounced back when their mines closed. They've become artist communities and tourist attractions. Why can't we do that here?"

The catcalls that greeted her statement grated against her nerves. Okay, so maybe that wasn't such a great idea after all, but she was only trying to protect her friends and neighbors. Eden was doing the right thing—she knew it.

She tried again. "I don't believe the word of any Kipling, especially one who is a stranger to our way of life. We have a right to question his motives and actions. How do we know he really wants the best for our community and not his own pocketbook?"

A low blow, but an effective one. Eden surveyed the room, glad to see she had most of the people's undivided attention. Around Jake she noticed a lot of the young men, some from neighboring towns, shutting her out. These were the ones she needed to reach.

"But what about jobs? It's easy for you, you have a business in town, while we have nothing." An old classmate spoke up, holding the hand of his wife. "I need a job. This man is offering one if the mine reopens."

"Here, here." The sound of several people clapping broke out, drowning out her response. If she couldn't get her point across, she had no hope of convincing the counsel to throw out Kipling's request. Eden contained her rising panic. She couldn't lose.

"Let her speak," Jake called out.

Eden was unable to deny the challenge anymore than she could keep her gaze from him. His crooked grin signaled the end of any attempt at a civil conversation.

The fliers were nothing. She had yet to begin.

"What about jobs?" Eden directed her question to the group of men sitting near Jake. "How can there be any jobs when there's nothing to mine? I remember the rumors floating around town before—before—don't you? He's wrong. He hasn't even done any new surveys; he said so himself. And if the town does grant his request, when he does do them, they'll show what the last survey did. There's not enough copper left in Mina de Cobre to produce a hundred thousand dollars, much less a million. The ore grade had been in decline for at least a year prior to the accident. The mine had been worked out. Nor is it safe. It wasn't safe twenty years ago."

"You're wrong, Eden." Out of the corner of her eye, she saw Jake jump off his chair and pace to her side. She spun around to face him. His nearness sent a jolt of current through her; the look in his eyes riveted her in her place. Somehow, this battle had moved to a personal level that had nothing to do with the mine. Around them, the spectators fell into an uneasy silence.

"Am I, Mr. Kipling?"

She turned to face the council again. "So what if there's ten billion dollars left? Reopening the mine is not the answer. Greta Reinhart, you lost your husband that day. Has twenty years dimmed the memory of that sweet man?"

Eden looked away in guilt as she saw Greta reach for a tissue out of her purse. She knew she was playing with the people's emotions, but Jake had left her with no choice.

Spying Juan Ybarra seated along the aisle, she walked over and knelt in front of him. "Mr. Ybarra, you lost your only son to that man's family." She picked up his unsteady hands and squeezed them. "Do you honestly think a few more customers in your barber chair is going to make up for that?"

Her heart wrenched in two as a broken sob echoed in her ears. She looked into the face of Juan's wife before pulling herself to her feet and walking back to the front.

"Mayor Clifford, we all lost our fathers due to Kipling negligence." Her voice cracked under the strain of her words, yet she persisted. She had to. No one else in town chose to speak for the dead men. "We had no fathers to play ball with, no fathers to teach us how to drive, no fathers to give us away at our weddings—"

"Enough, Eden," Abuelo said in a weary voice. "You've made your point, *Nieta*. Please sit down."

Her body shuddered from the surge of emotion, but her heart lay heavy inside her chest. Judging from the stillness of the gym, she'd made her point.

So why did it feel so wrong?

She inhaled deeply before finishing her speech. "Remember the day shift. How many more lives do you want to jeopardize for the sake of money?"

Pandemonium broke out.

Shouts erupted as tempers flared. Several of the younger men openly challenged the opposition to step forward. Women and children screamed as most of the town's residents scrambled for the exits when the pushing and shoving turned into an outright brawl. Eden saw Tyler radio for backup as he headed for the largest group of fighters.

"Oh, *Dios*, what have I done?" She groaned as she slunk toward the far wall, dodging paper projectiles. A chair crashed against the brick wall and fell to the floor, just shy of where she stood. She jumped.

Jake grabbed her around the waist and half carried her to the door. "Nice speech, Eden. Do you always go around inciting riots?"

Chapter Three

Outside in the waning heat, Jake released Eden. He really wanted to shake some sense into her for causing such a ruckus, but that wouldn't solve a thing. Besides, with all the people streaming out of the gym, somebody—though he couldn't imagine who, after her little escapade—would come to her rescue.

The sheriff's deputy came to mind since he and Eden seemed to have some kind of relationship. Jake was the bigger of the two men; still, he had no desire to take on a member of the law enforcement.

"I suppose you want me to thank you for saving my life again!" Eden retorted, folding her arms in a defensive position as she leaned against the brick wall of the building they'd just vacated.

Jake raised an eyebrow. Obviously, he'd been misinformed. Not all women liked being rescued. Next time he'd curb his protective streak around Eden if the need arose. "Oh, I don't doubt you would have made it out unharmed. A simple apology will do just fine."

"Apologize? Apologize for what? The truth?" The glint in her eyes equaled the conviction in her voice. "Everything I said in there was true. You may be able to fool the rest of the town with your overstated figures, Kipling, but you can't fool me."

He bit back a cynical reply. Since the number of people exiting had dwindled to nothing, he stepped back and studied her intently. For someone who barely came up to his shoulder, she was proving to be a huge obstacle. If only he could figure out what went on in that pretty head of hers.

Pretty? He should check himself into a psychiatric ward. He looked at her again. Dark eyes, too large for her face, overshadowed the high cheekbones that complimented her straight, pert nose. Her wide lips were perfect for pouting. Jake had no doubt she'd resort to that soon enough to get her way; all the women he'd known eventually did. Separately her features seemed out of proportion and out of place. Together, they were stunning. Even without makeup, he realized she was an incredible specimen of the opposite sex, even if she was a curvy brunette.

Too bad she was a local. Too bad the circumstances weren't different.

"First, I think you should apologize to the town for

your—your questionable behavior," he said. "Then I'd like to see those records you spoke about."

A fleeting sense of regret coursed through Eden. Jake's request shouldn't have surprised her. He'd rescued her again for questioning, not out of some deep-rooted sense of chivalry. Though his crisp, white shirt and gray pin-striped suit was a far cry from how she pictured her knight in shining armor. She was waiting for a man . . . a man like her father and Abuelo.

Eden sagged against the warm bricks. What was it about Jake Kipling that made her temper snap? Unable to face the intense expression on his face, she looked down, placed her heel in the dirt, and drew obscure patterns with her sandal.

"Well, do I get to see these records or not?" Jake asked, taking a step closer to her as a small group of men passed by. Eden didn't like his nearness, yet she held her position. Which wasn't easy with a wall at her back, Jake in front, and a concerto of crickets jarring her nerves. "Are these records real or were they just a ploy to keep the mine shut, Eden?

Eden's gaze flew to his, angered by his insinuations. Why, she'd—she'd ask the same questions if the roles were reversed. Her hostility dissipated into the still evening.

"They're real," she replied in a grudging voice. Knowing she'd done enough damage for one night, she had nothing to lose by showing him the figures. "Even after twenty years, they have to be more accurate than your preliminary analysis and your grandfather's notes. The dollar amounts you spoke about *are* overstated and inaccurate. Everyone knows it takes millions of years for the earth to produce copper. It doesn't show up overnight."

"It can if the surveys are wrong."

"They're not. I saw them yesterday."

"Then why doesn't the Department of Mines in Phoenix have a record of these so-called surveys?" he asked smoothly with no expression on his face.

Eden blinked. He didn't believe her. "I—I don't know. All I do know is what I saw, and it doesn't look very promising." And maybe, just maybe, after she showed him how dismal his prospects were, he'd pack up and leave. Then she'd have peace of mind again. "I'm director of the Mining Museum in the old depot on Main. Meet me there tomorrow at three and I'll show you the records."

All morning long, the topic at the diner revolved around the mine. People who normally ate at home stopped in for coffee to commend Eden on her speech. Others, however, were conspicuously absent.

Battle lines had been drawn and factions formed—whole families torn apart. Her brother, Adam, had barely spoken to her and Abuelo—a man of few words anyway—only asked enough questions to prepare the breakfast orders. Even Nana was unusually subdued.

She supposed it didn't matter. They'd see her point of view. They had to.

Eden sighed, emptying the last grounds from the coffee maker, glad the first part of her day was over. The worst still lay ahead of her. Replacing the filter tray, she grabbed a towel and cleaned the few drops of liquid underneath the machine. Then she attacked the counter, making sure it was spotless before she headed to the tables.

Leaning in to close the blinds on the front window, she spied Jake pacing by the museum door. She grimaced, glancing at her watch, which read a quarter to three. He must be anxious to see those records, she thought.

She sat down anyway, blew the wisps of bangs from her eyes, and rested her head against her fisted palm. The man was far too handsome for her tastes. Still, she could appreciate a good view. Too few men of his kind resided in Prosperity. Anyone with half a brain had moved to Tucson or Phoenix or beyond. Exactly where Jake would go when she showed him his dismal prospects.

The thought should have brought a smile to her lips, but she caught herself frowning. She continued staring at the man striding so purposely across the way even though she wasn't interested in him. Or, if she thought about it carefully, anyone else for that matter.

Had her father's death scarred her in more ways than she realized? Nonsense. She just hadn't met anyone to be interested in. And if she did, it would *not* be Mr. Jonathan Alexander Kipling.

The alarm on her watch toned three. "Darn it!" She jumped up and closed the blinds before she picked up the rag and ran to the counter to dump it in the bucket. As she grabbed the handle of the bucket to haul it back to the utility sink, the bells over the front door jingled. Eden looked up just in time to see Jake walk through. Her heart stalled.

"Hello, Eden. Mind if I wait in here until you're done? It's a little hot out there."

Of course she minded; she wasn't ready to face him yet, especially with her thoughts in such turmoil, but she wasn't insensitive enough to torture the man and make him wait outside. A light sheen of perspiration had gathered on his forehead just from the few minutes he'd been out there. "Um. Sure. Have a seat." She gestured toward the far table, hoping that if he sat at a distance, she'd be able to regain her composure. "Can I get you a soda or something? I shouldn't be too much longer."

"Water would be great. Thanks."

Instead of sitting at the table, to her dismay, he occupied a stool at the counter, right next to where she'd been working when he walked through the door. Eden placed the glass in front of him and reached for the bucket.

"May I make a suggestion?"

She eyed him uncertainly, not quite sure whether

she wanted to hear his proposition no matter how sincere he looked. Common sense prevailed. "What?"

"Why don't you go change, and I'll finish whatever needs to be done here."

Eden didn't have to think twice about it. "Fine. This gets dumped in the back sink," she said, pointing to the bleach water. "And the rag goes into the cloth bag next to it. The broom to sweep the floor is in the closet off to the right. I'll be back in five minutes."

Four minutes and fifty-five seconds later, Eden rejoined Jake as he swept the last bit of dirt into the dustpan and dumped it into the garbage can. Scanning the floor, Eden was surprised to see he'd done an adequate job. More then adequate, actually. It looked like he'd even picked up the mats behind the counter and swept under them too. Something she only did every few days or so.

"Unbelievable," Jake said, looking first at his watch, then at her. "I think you just set a new world record."

"What's that supposed to mean?" Eden stopped reaching for her purse, which she'd stashed on the shelf under the cash register, and stood, facing him.

"I've never known a woman who could get ready so fast." He gave her a crooked grin as he leaned on the handle of the broom. "They usually like to keep me waiting an hour or so before they appear."

"Well," she retorted as she slung the purse strap over her shoulder, "I'm obviously not like other women you know." She shrugged. "Besides, it's not like this is a date or anything. I don't even like you. Put the broom away and I'll shut off the cooler and the lights."

Turning quickly to avoid his response, she locked the cash register then ushered Jake out of the diner and followed after him. As she locked the door, she looked both ways down Main. Deserted. Nothing to keep her from delaying the inevitable. Once Jake saw the surveys, he'd be out of here quicker than snow in July.

"It's quite a structure. When was it built?" Jake stopped at the curb and pointed to the depot.

"1903." Her gaze strayed to the building. "It's hard to believe the old depot was once the crowning glory of Prosperity." Her mind wandered for a moment and she spoke more to herself than the man next to her. "I can still see the big engine and hear the whistle blow before the train pulled out. When the mine closed, the trains stopped . . ."

"Because there was no reason for them to come here anymore." Kipling finished the sentence for her.

She didn't like that. Not one bit.

"Yes. Lucky for us, instead of closing it when he left, your grandfather *sold* it to the town, along with the general store and several miners' houses." Eden couldn't keep the venom from her voice.

She stole a glance at Jake. His jaw tensed for a second, but relaxed. Obviously, he chose not to acknowledge her dig against his grandfather because his tone was even, almost friendly, when he replied. "And then you converted it into the museum."

She followed his lead. Arguing would get them nowhere. "My mother started it, then Mrs. Jackson continued on after she died. I helped her, then took over when I was sixteen." The museum was Eden's baby, her pride and joy. One of the few places she felt close to her father. She sighed, taking a good look at the place. "It sure could use a face-lift."

One of the wooden beams supporting the porch roof was bowed, the ruddy brown brick was crumbled in places, and many of the tiles were broken or missing. Most of the original thick-paned windows had been replaced by newer, thinner versions, creating a dysfunctional, pieced-together look.

"This town could use a lot of things, Eden. Without an infusion of money, the depot, along with a number of other old structures lining Main, will deteriorate beyond repair."

"Prosperity needs something, but the mine *isn't* the answer." Tired of standing in the heat, Eden jumped off the curb and walked into the street, thankful Brandon and the boys had found some other place to play ball today.

"Then what is?" Jake joined her instantly, her stride no match for his, no matter how big her step.

"I still think we should advertise for more tourists like other defunct mining towns. Look at Bisbee and

Jerome. Once the artists moved in and reclaimed the towns, they created a booming business."

"With the town in the shape that it's in? I think you'll have a hard time attracting anyone until the buildings are repaired. How do you propose to do that?"

"I'll do it myself, if I have to," she answered as she climbed the stairs and walked across the porch. The fact that Jake had a point rattled her. All the buildings in town needed renovation.

Eden slipped a key into the metal lock of the thick, wooden door. The sound of the deadbolt sliding open resounded in her ears. With her hand flat on the coarse wood surface, she forced the heavy museum door open.

As her sight adjusted from the bright sunshine, she flipped on lights, trying to dispel the dim atmosphere. "Here we are. Are you sure you still want to see how dismal your prospects are?"

"Of course." Jake's vibrant voice filled the cramped area. "Interesting place. Though it doesn't look like anyone's been here for a while. Do you get many visitors?"

"No. But I still maintain the records and photographs in memory of my father and the other miners killed."

She glanced around the filthy room as Jake had done, glad the dimness hid the flush in her cheeks. Yesterday, she'd been too focused on reviewing the old records to notice her housekeeping skills had waned over the summer. A healthy layer of dust covered everything. She was afraid to breathe too deeply for fear she'd sneeze and upset more than dust. Judging from what she hoped were cricket droppings on the flagstone floor, she'd have to prevail on Mr. Rudford's exterminating services again.

Eden switched on the cooling unit, then walked over and pulled the string connected to the rickety fan overhead and sent the blades turning before she swung her gaze to the narrow wooden desk in the corner. Behind it sat rows and rows of old, scratched, and dented file cabinets her mother had saved after the mining offices closed.

"How about a nickel tour since we're here?" Jake questioned softly. The moment they'd stepped into the museum, he somehow felt a closeness with his father, if that at all was possible, and wanted to prolong the visit. Or maybe it was the woman who stood in front of him. He wasn't sure anymore.

She gave him an inquisitive look but agreed. "Sure."

The scent of her perfume drifted under his nose as she stepped past him. Heady and floral, it enveloped Jake, bringing a comforting image of his mother to mind. But Mary Kipling was soft and sweet. Aside from wearing the same fragrance, the two women were as opposite as the sun and moon. Still, he was finding Eden more attractive each minute.

Keeping uninvolved with the locals was going to be

tougher than he'd imagined, but he had to do it. His mother hadn't, and look what happened to her.

"Here's the mine on opening day in 1902." Eden drew his attention back to the first of a series of faded black-and-white photographs hung on the wall.

Jake was glad for the distraction. Her effect on him disturbed his sense of balance. He moved past her and aligned himself in front of the pictures, creating a false sense of distance. Questions concerning the mine needed answers, not inquiries into this—this whatever it was that lingered between them. He tried to block out Eden's existence and focused on the old headframe of the original shaft and the smelters set close by.

"You know that nothing from this era remains, except for what's been preserved in the museum." Her voice was distant even though she'd moved in to stand next to him. "The buildings your grandfather didn't sell, he dismantled in order to avoid property taxes."

For once, Jake couldn't fault his grandfather for this decision. "I doubt that was his only reason. Aside from the taxes, the old buildings could have become a hazard to the community and an invitation to trouble. Replacing them will be costly, but worth the expense when the mine is operational."

"*If* the mine is operational. Which it won't be."

Jake ignored her statement as he fingered the lobe of his ear. He hadn't been able to break himself of the habit even though he'd taken the rebellious earring out years ago. "The industry has come a long way since this was taken. Technologies available today have made it possible to extract ore that wasn't economically feasible twenty years ago."

"Too bad you won't have a chance to use these new technologies here, Mr. Kipling. There's nothing left." This time, her comment couldn't be overlooked. Her triumphant voice eroded part of his confidence.

He'd been wrong once before, but his gut feeling told him he wasn't wrong about this. As soon as the town approved his request and he had access to bring in equipment, he would prove there was enough copper to make it feasible to operate the mine.

"So you say, but I won't believe it until all the numbers are in."

He stepped away and continued to look around the museum. Shelves containing numerous volumes of mining and mineral books bowed under their weight while old equipment lay piled haphazardly along the baseboards and hung on the off-white walls. But it was the transparent cases in the center of the room that grabbed his attention.

"What's in here?" Jake stopped by the first glass display box and blew a thin layer of dust off the surface.

"Scrips," Eden answered as she stepped in beside him and cleaned off the rest of the surface with a rag she'd found somewhere. The rag wasn't much cleaner than the glass, but at least it would rearrange the dirt for the time being.

Next to what looked like an old letter from the United States Treasury was a row of coins, each about the size of a half dollar, displayed on a piece of royal blue velvet. Eden lifted the glass cover, retrieved a coin, and handed it to him.

"The infamous scrips." He analyzed the aluminum coin intently. On one side 'Mina de Cobra, Prosperity, Arizona' was inscribed around the border and the center stamped with 'One Dollar' and a small 'In Trade' placed under the amount. The back was imprinted with 'Kipling Copper Corporation' and the family crest.

"My mother told me they were issued as a courtesy to the miners in the forties, kind of as a cash advance. Of course by payday, sometimes the men wouldn't have anything left and would receive zero checks. The practice stopped when the government learned about it. Otherwise, I bet half the town would still be indebted to your family."

Jake heard the edge return to her voice and had no doubt that her expression had turned to stone again. He couldn't see though, because she'd spun away from him and walked straight to the desk. Gently he placed the coin back in the case, lowered the lid, and followed her.

"Now, did you want to see those files or not?" Eden pulled out the middle drawer in the filing cabinet and began rifling through the well-used manila folders. Over the ruffling sound, Jake heard her curse quietly.

"What's wrong?"

She didn't answer him right away. Instead she slammed the drawer shut, then opened the one above it. As he peered over her shoulder, Jake scanned the file labels. None were titled anything close to what they were looking for, unless Eden had a unique filing system.

"They're not here." Jake heard the frustration in her voice as Eden closed that drawer and leaned her head against the scratched surface. "I don't understand it. I saw them yesterday. Right here." She yanked out the middle drawer and searched the files again.

An uneasy feeling settled in Jake's stomach. Surely she had more to gain by showing the surveys to him. Had they been a fabrication on Eden's part after all? Would she stoop that low to keep the mine shut?

The look on her face when she turned to face him convinced him that unless she was a great actress, the surveys did exist. But at the same time, he was certain she was lying about something. He'd noticed her hesitation, slight as it was. He'd been lied to before, and it had cost him and his company a lot of money. Jake wouldn't let that happen again, no matter what. So why was he giving her the benefit of the doubt?

Because he was a sucker for chocolate-brown eyes.

"It's okay, Eden—"

"No. It's not okay. I promised you those files and, unlike a Kipling, a Delgado never goes back on a promise. They have to be here somewhere."

For a moment, Jake bristled at her direct assault—

until he thought about his grandfather, Charles. Somehow he wasn't surprised the old man had never followed through on whatever he'd promised the town. Jake himself knew all too well what it felt like. Charles hadn't bothered to go see his only grandson hit a grand slam during the final playoff game that had led his high school team to victory.

To this day he kept telling himself that it didn't matter. But it did. Jake took a deep breath, caught a whiff of Eden's perfume, and thought of his mother again. At least Mary had cared, and he was thankful he took after her, not his grandfather.

Starting tomorrow, he'd make sure a Kipling never broke another promise to Eden or the people of Prosperity. "The records are here somewhere, Eden. You've just misplaced them. I can wait until you find them."

Chapter Four

"They've come back, Daddy," Eden spoke to the gray marble slab in the corner of the Prosperity cemetery. She visited every week, regardless of the weather. In the summer, that just meant getting there before the sun edged it's way over Sumner's Peak. She sat motionless for a moment and drank in the pale scent of morning. All too soon, the sun would rise and snuff out the earthy perfume and replace it with the heat of early September.

Grabbing the set of gloves tucked in her back pocket she pulled them on, knelt, and began tugging at the weeds near the headstone. For twenty years she'd come to talk to her father, even though it made her miss him more.

Thanks to the Kiplings, this was all she had left.

An image of Jake Kipling wavered in her mind. His strength and protectiveness attracted her. So did his deep blue eyes. Disloyalty stabbed at her as she piled the wilting weeds next to the headstone. How could she even think about the possibilities?

She wouldn't. Her hands clenched into fists. Her father deserved better.

"They want to reopen the mine. But I'm not going to let them. The town is in an uproar; everyone is fighting. Even Adam hasn't talked to me. After what happened, how could anyone even consider—oh, Daddy, I miss you so much."

Overwhelmed with the events of the past few days, Eden's eyes filled with tears as she knelt there, silently tracing her father's name carved in the stone with her index finger. The solid rock offered a comfort she hadn't felt in days. Aside from her memories and a few relics at home and the museum, this was all she had left.

Wiping away the moisture, Eden heard the birds sing their way into morning as she shifted her attention from the simple granite marker to the whitewashed adobe chapel shaded by an old ironwood tree. Beside the stone steps, a rabbit bounded across the grass and escaped under the fence. Her gaze traveled the length of the chipped, white wood to the end and beyond. Not only had the town suffered from neglect and time, so had the cemetery.

The sputtering sound of a lawn mower turning over

broke the silence. Eden glanced over her shoulder and saw the caretaker, Mr. Kelly, fiddling with the mower. He yanked the cord again and this time the engine jumped to life. Eden waved, but Mr. Kelly didn't see her. At eighty-five, his eyesight was about as good as his edging skills. He started cutting the sparse grass around the headstones.

Since her visits usually coincided with his, Eden knew Mr. Kelly always started with the older section of the cemetery. Probably out of respect. Underneath the bleached, crumbling marble lay the town founders—ancestors of the citizens of today. Eden hadn't known them personally, but she knew them well, having documented the history of the town as well as the mine. She knew everyone from cradle to grave.

"None of the Kiplings are here," she muttered. Her chin rose a fraction at the intentional slight. Prosperity had made them rich, yet instead of lying alongside the folks who made them their fortune, the high and mighty Kiplings were buried in a mausoleum back East. New York, to be exact.

Which is exactly where she wished Jake Kipling would go.

Finished with her father's plot, Eden worked silently on her grandfather's, then her uncle's. When the wiry old man pushing the lawn mower began to mow the section next to her, Eden shouted to be heard over the din, "Good morning, Mr. Kelly."

The caretaker cut the engine and peace descended again.

"Good morning to you too, Eden. How's the family?" he asked, taking the battered Arizona Cardinals hat from his balding head and wiping his brow.

"As well as can be expected, Mr. Kelly. I talk and they listen." Eden found a smile tugging at the corners of her mouth. She and the caretaker had this conversation every week, yet this time it added a bit of normalcy to her life—something that had been missing since Jake Kipling stormed into town.

"Beautiful mornin' ain't it?" As Mr. Kelly stretched his arms over his head, Eden heard his bones crack. The sound echoed in the still morning.

"Yes it is. I heard you were ill; how are you feeling today?"

"Tired, but better. Glad I'm still here—'bove ground, that is."

Eden joined in as Mr. Kelly laughed. His humor was contagious. "I'm glad."

"So'm I, although others ain't quite so pleased."

Her smile turned upside down. "We missed you at the meeting the other night, but Mrs. Kelly did us proud. She sure put Mr. Kipling in his place." Eden had been ready to applaud when Mrs. Kelly accused the Kipling family of breaking their promise. The caretaker and his wife, along with the other families, should know. Mr. and Mrs. Kelly's only grandson perished along with Eden's father and the others in the cave-in. "I see Mrs. Kelly is using a walker now. How's her hip doing?"

"It bothered her this morning, but not as much as this whole mining issue. The missus cain't understand why this Kipling has come back. Or why the town is backing him."

"That makes two of us." Eden followed his gaze toward the mine in the distance. Even after twenty years, the natural vegetation had scarcely begun to cover the scars in the mountainside. As the sun edged over the peaks, tiny shafts of light danced on the old tailings. No matter where she looked, what she thought of, or what she did these days, everything reflected back to the mine. Once it was the lifeblood of town, but no longer.

"Why are there so few of us who can see the truth, Mr. Kelly?" Eden still sat crouched down near the headstone of her uncle's grave. In her agitation, she had pulled out more clumps of weeds and grass than necessary to clear the space around the marble. Now a bare section of ground remained and she could see the life wilt out of the grass that had barely clung to life anyway in the dry region.

"I dunno, child. I dunno." With that, Mr. Kelly attempted to start the old lawn mower again, but nothing happened when he pulled the cord. "Dang thing burns up gas like there's no tomorrow," Mr. Kelly grumbled as he slapped the rusted handle. "Guess I'd better run to town if I wanna get finished 'fore the heat sets in."

Mr. Kelly left and Eden replanted the withering grass. Satisfied, she batted loose the dirt from her gloves and tended to her mother's plot until the creaking sound of the gate caught her attention. Expecting the caretaker, she turned in time to see Jake Kipling secure the lock.

What was he doing here? And why did he look around as if making sure no one else was about? Half-hidden by the headstone and a mesquite tree, Eden couldn't decide what to do. Should she make herself known? Or wait until he left?

Nature took the decision out of her hands. She sneezed.

Surprised, Jake swung his attention toward the sound. He'd hoped the cemetery would be deserted this time of day so he could fulfill part of his mother's dying request. But he had to do so in secret. He couldn't take the chance of discovery. Not yet.

At first glance he didn't see anybody, but partially hidden to his right sat Eden. The last person he wanted to run into. He hadn't seen or heard from her since the museum, though ignoring her when they found themselves in the same area wasn't a gentlemanly thing to do. People had accused him of various things, but they'd never accused him of being rude. She waved tentatively as he approached.

"Good morning, Eden." Jake spoke first to break the uncomfortable silence.

"Good morning, Mr. Kipling."

His attention strayed downward in an attempt to escape her inquisitive look. Mistake. Jake couldn't take his eyes off her. No matter what she wore, she was still sexy. He swallowed hard. Her cut-off jeans and her T-shirt clung to her curves. On her hands she wore a pair of dirt-encrusted men's work gloves, the only part of her anatomy properly covered.

He thought about returning later to finish his errand.

"What are you doing here?" Eden finally uttered the question mirrored in her eyes. Another wave of attraction rolled over him. Jake wondered if her voice was always so low and throaty in the morning.

He would've loved to discover that enticing piece of information if she'd been someone else. But she wasn't, and thanks to his mother's 'transgressions', as Charles had called them, he was determined never to find out.

Jake tried to respond with a believable answer that had nothing to do with the truth. He couldn't, so in desperation he changed the subject. "I'm sure you're aware the council approved the access."

A bitter expression crossed Eden's face before she tilted her head down. Her brown hair cascaded around her face, muffling her reply. "Of course. The Kipling family always gets what it wants."

Ready to take offense, Jake struggled to keep calm. Eden had spoken the truth. The Kiplings had usually gotten what they'd wanted because they had the name, the money, and the power. But that was all. They had never truly been a family in the literal sense of the word.

"Not always."

One look at the well-tended headstones and Jake knew Eden was fiercely loyal and protective of her family. A sudden longing to turn her loyalties around enveloped him. For purely business reasons he told himself—nothing more. If he could convince Eden the mine *was* the viable answer to the town's current financial problems, he was sure the rest of the opposition would follow.

As Eden sat back on her heels, she wiped a stray hair from her face. The motion, innocent enough, sent another wave of longing through him. "I find that hard to believe." She leaned over to collect her tools, then stood and said in a breathless whisper that stirred his blood again, "I've got to get to work."

"Well then, don't work too hard."

After she left, Jake waited a few minutes to make sure he was completely alone in the cemetery. Once certain, he retraced his steps to the backpack left inconspicuously by the gate. Then he walked toward another headstone placed not far from Eden's family and squatted to place a small metal trinket by its corner.

Standing at the front door of the Kipling mansion, Eden hesitated. She knew exactly the last time she'd been here—even without the faded photograph in her mother's photo album. The date, the time, and what she'd worn were as fresh in her mind as if it had happened yesterday, not almost twenty-one years ago. Christmas Eve, four o'clock in the afternoon, wearing a dark green velvet dress with white satin ribbons.

The garment had once belonged to her friend, Diana, but Eden hadn't cared. Her mother had altered it enough so that nobody would notice. Plus, she'd had matching ribbons laced through her braids and a shiny new pair of black patent leather shoes and a matching purse.

Her outfit for this evening had been a hand-me-down too. But from a stranger. Diana had convinced her to buy the black dress at the consignment shop last time they were in Bisbee. At the time, Eden had no idea where she'd wear the simple yet elegant dress, but never in her wildest dreams had she imagined it would be here.

"Ring the bell, Eden," her brother, Adam, said as he moved in beside her and adjusted his tie. Eden knew they were overdressed for the occasion, but Lori, who stood next to Adam, had insisted they wear their best clothes.

Taking a deep breath, she squared her shoulders and pushed the round, lighted button. The door opened instantly as if Jake had been waiting for them.

"Hello, Mr. Kipling."

"Miss Delgado." Jake hid his surprise well, though Eden could see his questioning look as he shook her hand.

So what if he'd given her more time to find those records that had mysteriously disappeared. So what if he had a seductive smile, an irresistible charm, and the sexiest blue eyes she'd ever seen. Jonathan Alexander Kipling was and would always be her enemy.

Or would he?

Light-headed, she leaned forward, gripping Jake's hand a little tighter. His arm wrapped protectively around her shoulders as he gathered her close so she wouldn't fall over.

"Are you okay? Can I get you something to drink?"

That would teach Eden not to eat all day. Feeling foolish, she regained her composure as the blood returned to her head. "A drink would be nice, thank you. And food would be appreciated too."

As they turned to enter the mansion, Eden remembered the other couple as she extracted herself from Kipling's hold. "I'm fine now, thank you. Have you met my brother, Adam, and my sister-in-law, Lori?"

"Pleased to meet you Adam, Lori. Welcome."

He ushered them inside and motioned for Adam and Lori to walk ahead of them. Once her brother and sister-in-law were out of earshot, Kipling stopped Eden and spoke under his breath. "Please behave yourself tonight, okay?"

Eden didn't take offense to his words because of her previous actions, which were not a true reflection of her personality. But he didn't know that. Flipping a stray lock of hair behind her shoulders, she gave him a tentative smile. "Of course, Mr. Kipling. I wouldn't dream of causing a scene here. Now, where's the food?"

"Allow me."

Taking a firm hold on her arm, Jake escorted her into the dining hall where the party was in full swing. Music and voices ebbed and flowed with the current topic around town. The mine. Which was what she expected, as she found herself gulping the contents of a soda glass Jake had placed in her hand.

The house still looked the same. Even twenty years hadn't diminished the grandeur of the old place, although the weather had aged the exterior and the landscaping had been neglected. Eden knew that Edgar Kipling, Charles's father, had built the place in 1906, and that it was made of adobe block made right on the property.

The mansion had been a present to his wife Margaret on her twenty-eighth birthday. Unfortunately, she'd died in childbirth along with her infant daughter six months after it had been completed. Rumor had it the old man had never been the same and, neither had his son, Charles Kipling, Jake's grandfather. But that was no excuse for Jake's poor behavior.

Eden backed away from the room full of people after grabbing a plate of food. The inside of the house seemed smaller than she remembered, and not quite as cheerful. An air of neglect had pervaded the interior too. The place was clean enough, but even the scent of cleaning solutions barely masked the musty odor. The wood of what little furniture had been left was dull, and the curtains lining the bay windows had faded to a nondescript beige.

Gulping the soda, she wandered into another room and over to the portrait wall of the deceased Kiplings. Edgar Kipling and Charles Kipling stared unsmiling back at her. She cringed and suddenly felt out of place, as if she were trespassing.

"Their eyes seem to follow you, don't they?" Jake questioned quietly in her ear. Eden clamped a hand over her mouth to keep from screaming. She hadn't heard him enter.

"Sorry, I didn't mean to frighten you."

Right, she thought, knowing he had every intention of taking her by surprise. He could have easily announced his presence at the doorway instead of slipping in next to her.

Willing her heartbeat to slow down, Eden stepped away and pointed to the empty spot on the wall. "Is that where the picture of your father used to hang?"

She saw Jake hesitate for a moment. "That's where my picture will go. Would you like to see the rest of the house?"

He turned and ushered her through the door. Eden didn't resist, knowing well enough that she'd stepped over some line that she hadn't even known was drawn. Why should Jake be so upset at the mention of his father?

Eden followed him silently up the hardwood stairs. She'd never been this far up into the house. Nobody she knew had ever ventured this far. She stopped in her tracks.

"What's wrong?" He must have seen the look of panic in her eyes, or heard the sound of her heart racing at light speed.

"I can't go any further."

"My grandfather is dead: he won't hurt you anymore. Come on, I have something to show you."

Charles may not hurt me, but what about you? She grabbed the hand he held out and somehow found the energy to climb up the spiral flight of stairs.

They bypassed several closed doors, stopping by the one at the far end of the hall. Eden's sense of direction wasn't that good, but she suspected they were about to enter the formidable tower. She shuddered, remembering stories from her childhood about the Kiplings keeping tabs of the townspeople from this very room. They'd always seemed to know everything.

In the dimness, Jake released her hand to use both of his to jiggle the copper handle. The door creaked open, setting Eden's teeth on edge and her skin crawling. Once inside, Jake nudged the door with his shoulder, shutting out the noise of the party below them before he flipped the switch.

As the lights drove away the darkness, Eden's mouth dropped open in amazement. Beautiful and ornate, yet comfortable, the room—a library of sorts—

took her breath away. More books than she could read in a lifetime lined the walls.

It was all Eden could do not to run to the shelves and run her fingers along the leather, gold-stamped bindings. The only thing that stopped her was the old set of binoculars sitting on the antique table by the lone window that dominated the room.

The stories were true.

"Come over here." Jake's voice beckoned softly. She stepped in beside him as the last of the sun's rays filtered through the glass pane. From the tower, Eden could see the entire town of Prosperity on the left, and the mine on the right.

"The town is dying, Eden. Can't you see it?"

She gazed down upon the deserted streets in the dusk, knowing the darkness would be heavier than normal since most of the town was at the party. In her head, Eden knew Jake spoke the truth, yet her heart refused to listen.

"I know there's years of copper left in those shafts. If I can prove it's a viable mine, will you stop fighting me?"

Eden made the mistake of looking into his sapphire eyes. Hope, ambition, and desire blazed from them. Jake really believed he could make this work. How would he feel when his dreams were nothing but a pile of dust ready to be scattered at the whim of a breeze—or in her case, a family?

"Even if there's millions of tons of copper left in

there, which I doubt there is, can you guarantee another man won't die in there?"

Jake swallowed, thrusting a hand through his blond hair. He whispered, "You know I can't promise that, Eden. It would be a lie. No matter how hard we try, mining is still a dangerous profession. Even with the advances since the turn of the century, accidents happen."

Eden stood there quietly for what seemed an eternity, watching the last of the sun's rays disappear over the far mountain range as his words echoed in her ears.

The exasperation in his voice told her more than his actual words. He saw dollar signs instead of individuals, profit margins instead of families, return on investments instead of a community.

The town might be dying a slow and painful death. But it was nothing compared to the sorrow and grief she still carried in her heart. Nothing could replace what the Kiplings had taken from her. Nothing.

"Yes, Mr. Kipling. Accidents happen," she replied, trying to keep the bitterness from her voice. But before she could turn away, he wrapped his hand around her waist and pulled her close.

"I've got an errand Monday that concerns the mine. Will you come with me?"

"No."

"Meet me outside the diner at four o'clock in the morning. You won't be sorry."

"Don't count on it," she replied breathlessly, escaped from his grasp, and ran out the door.

Chapter Five

"Good morning, Eden. Glad you decided to join me today," Jake said as he held the sport utility vehicle's door open for her. Even half asleep, Eden knew she was crazy to go along with his scheme. Four in the morning was just way too early for her. Normally she slept until at least five-thirty, if not later, usually arriving at the diner minutes before they unlocked the door at six.

"Morning, Mr. Kipling. I'm only here today because I want to persuade you not to reopen Mina de Cobre," Eden stated drowsily, settling herself in the dark leather seat.

"What a pity. And I thought you were here because of my magnetic personality." He winked at her broadly as he shut the door and sauntered to the driver's side.

"I didn't know the Kiplings had such a sense of humor." She looked at him through her lashes as he joined her in the white Lincoln Navigator. "Where are we going?"

Instead of answering, he threw the vehicle in gear, pulled out of the community parking lot, and turned west.

"Why all the secrecy?"

"It's no secret, Eden. I'm going to prove to you that the copper exists."

"But the mine is in the other direction." Bewildered, Eden rubbed her eyes, hoping that action would erase the cobwebs from her mind. Because she'd dozed after the alarm sounded, she'd barely had time to dress, much less brew a pot of coffee. A definite oversight if she wanted to make sense of Jake's actions.

"I'm well aware of that. We'll be going there soon enough. Right now, we're headed to Tucson."

"Tucson?" She gasped in shock. Was he out of his mind? Waking from her daze, she turned to face him. His gaze was on the stretch of road illuminated by the headlights, but she sensed his attention lay elsewhere. "Why are we going to Tucson? That's miles from here. I have all the records in Prosperity. I just need more time to locate them."

"You'll find out when we get there. Now just sit back and enjoy the ride. Would you like a cup of coffee?" Jake gestured to the thermos at her feet. How

Eden had missed the metal container, complete with cup, was beyond her, but she welcomed its presence.

Enjoy the ride? Right!

Now, coffee on the other hand . . . Eden retrieved the thermos and poured herself some of the hot, aromatic brew. It scalded her tongue, but she continued to sip after blowing lightly across the dark surface. She wanted—no, needed—the caffeine to help her make sense of everything. If there was anything to make sense of. Eden wondered if they were on a wild goose chase through southern Arizona.

Shifting in the seat, she was glad to see that Kipling had had enough sense to place woven Mexican blankets over the posh gray leather. Later in the day, when the blazing heat replaced the cool morning air, leather had an obnoxious way of gathering sweat where it came in contact with skin no matter how high the air conditioning blasted.

The Navigator had that new vehicle smell, leather and plastic, mingling with the heady masculine scent of Jake. This was insane. Tucson was over two hours away. It would probably take them all day to find whatever tiny shred of evidence he wanted, then a two-hour ride home. She'd never make it back in time to—to what? Watch *Jeopardy* on TV?

Eden slumped back, realizing her social life amounted to nothing except watching game shows and reruns when her head wasn't buried in a book. She didn't even particularly like *Jeopardy*. When she did manage to phrase the answer in a question correctly, her elation was short-lived. The show reminded her of all she'd missed by quitting her studies after high school.

She peeked at Jake, imagining him standing behind the contestant podium dressed in his suit. Surely a graduate of Harvard, or Yale, or whatever preppy school he'd attended, would do well at answering those trivial questions no one but the contestants gave a hoot about.

"Where'd you go to school?" she suddenly asked.

"That depends." He tilted his head sideways enough to look at her, yet still kept his attention on the road. "According to my grandfather, I attended the engineering school at Yale—"

"Figures," Eden muttered under her breath. She'd been right in assuming he'd attended an Ivy League school. The Kiplings had to have the best money could buy. Except when it came to the safety at the mine.

"What figures?"

"Oh, nothing."

"Then why did you ask?"

At a loss for words, she plucked at a loose thread in the blanket beneath her. "I—I was curious. That's all."

Jake applied the brakes and pulled off to the side of the county highway. After he placed the vehicle in park, he turned his full attention on her. "I didn't graduate from Yale. Charles never recognized the fact that I dropped out to finish my degree at the Colorado School of Mines."

A faraway expression settled across his face, but in a blink of an eye, it vanished. "We do come from opposite worlds—in some ways—but we're really not as different as you think we are, Eden. We both want what we think is best for the town, and our stubborn attitudes will probably cause unnecessary heartache not only to ourselves, but those around us."

"I don't think—" Eden started to contradict him, but she knew he spoke the truth. Well, half-truth. He was the one with the stubborn attitude, not her.

"Let me finish, Eden. As for my schooling, having money and a college education doesn't make a person." Gently, he picked up her palm, extended her fingers, and guided them over the thin white fabric covering her heart. "It's what's inside here," he moved her hand so that her fingers touched her left temple, "and here that counts. You may not think you have anything, but you have it all. My grandfather was one of the richest men in New York. When he died, he was a lonely, bitter old man."

Jake dropped her hand, threw the Navigator into drive, and sped off. Eden didn't know what to say. What had he meant when he said she had it all? Right now she had nothing. Finishing the coffee in her cup, she closed her eyes to ponder that thought.

She must have slept, lulled to sleep by the steady

motion of the vehicle, because when she opened her eyes, they were on the outskirts of Tucson, turning into a small regional airport.

"The airport? Why on earth—" Eden felt like a fish out of water as she struggled to suck in oxygen. She figured she must look like one too; her eyes had to be round as saucers, her mouth open wide, gasping for air as she exited the Navigator.

Walking across what Jake called the tarmac, Eden faltered a step. If he hadn't caught her by the elbow, she didn't doubt she'd be face down on the concrete. Still she wished he'd remove his hand. His touch sent jolts of current through her body that had nothing to do with what appeared to be her upcoming flight.

"Where are we going, Mr. Kipling?"

"You'll see." He steered her toward a small plane with high wings and a propeller at the front. As they approached, two men stepped forward.

"Good morning, Jake." The tall, dark-haired man dressed in khaki pants and navy blue polo shirt spoke first. "Hello. You must be Eden. I'm Robert Fornier, Jake's partner-in-crime from New York. I'm pleased to finally get to meet you," he murmured, gently raising her hand to his lips. Eden blushed fiercely at his forward approach and wondered if the East Coast always bred such attractive men. Not that she had much experience with anyone outside of Cochise County, much less another state. Too bad he was on the same side as Jake.

"Good morning, Robert," she replied quickly as the grip on her arm tightened. Eden glanced up at Jake and withdrew her hand after she caught the murderous expression on his face. Confusion clouded her thinking, but before she could utter a word the older gentleman wearing well-worn army fatigues held out his hand. "Good morning, Mr. and Mrs. Kipling. I'm Bill Watson, your pilot. Welcome aboard."

"But I'm not—"

"Good morning, Bill. Call me Jake. Come along, Eden." Jake cut her off as he led her to the plane. "These things have no air conditioning and I want to be back before the thermals and the heat of the day set in."

Eden wasn't too sure about the whole situation. Anticipation mingled with apprehension. Flying had been a childhood fantasy. Day after day she'd lifted her arms and flapped them, dreaming of soaring with the birds. Of course, those were just silly daydreams, something she'd never given much thought about after the accident. But today it looked like her dream was going to come true, whether she liked it or not.

Eyeing the white airplane with the orange stripe painted across the side, she wasn't sure this thing could get off the ground. Eden had always thought planes were so much . . . bigger. As she peered in the open door, the interior looked no roomier than the Navigator they'd just left parked in the lot. "What kind of plane is this?"

"It's a Cessna 206. Haven't you ever seen one?"

"No." Eden wiped her damp palms on the front of her tan shorts and took a deep breath before she admitted, "To be honest with you, I've never flown before."

She turned in time to see Jake regard her with a look she couldn't decipher. "In that case, you can have the front seat," he said, handing her off to Bill, who waited patiently inside the plane.

Stooping so she wouldn't hit her head on the roof, Eden settled herself into the right seat. The plane still didn't feel any bigger than the Navigator. In fact, it felt smaller as both Jake and Robert seated themselves.

"Fasten your seatbelt, Eden," Jake said. "Do know how to do it? Or do you need some help?"

Eden looked at the straps hanging off the seat and breathed a sigh of relief. The belts were like the ones in Abuelo's old Chevy. "Of course." With a snap, she secured herself onto the seat and waited for the adventure—she couldn't find another word to describe their outing—to begin.

"Here." Bill handed her a headset. "Put this on before we take off, this is how we'll communicate. It gets awful noisy in here during flight. Jake, Robert's already given me our G.P.S position; do you have any further instructions?"

"None at all," Eden heard Jake answer as he settled in his seat.

"What's a G.P.S. system?" Eden questioned, confused at the jargon they tossed around.

"It stands for Global Positioning System, which is a satellite system used for flight navigation. I punch in the longitude and latitude into this contraption here on the yoke," Bill pointed to a black box mounted on a Y-shaped steering wheel, "and it lets me know when we've reached our position. Now, is everyone buckled in?"

Suddenly, the propeller roared to life. Eden jumped. Then she remembered the headset in her hands and placed it over her ears. The noise decreased immediately. When the plane began to move, the sensation was like a moving car, so she relaxed—a little. Her hands remained balled into fists on her lap and butterflies gathered in her stomach, but for the first time in a long time, she felt alive—really truly alive.

With a new sense of confidence, she took interest in her surroundings. The plane may be small, but it was about to open up a whole new world for her. One she didn't want to miss any part off, so she leaned forward to see as much as she could. They taxied past a row of hangars, then a small brick building and onto the beginning of the runway before it stopped. Why were they stopping? Eden tore her gaze away from the window to look at the pilot.

"Just running the engine up, ma'am." Bill saluted her with two fingers and announced his intentions over the microphone. Then he adjusted some of the knobs on the console and the plane sped forward, the force pushing Eden back into her seat.

As the Cessna ate up the long stretch of concrete, the hangars to her left and natural desert landscaping to her right whizzed by. It almost made her dizzy. But when the bumpy sensation smoothed out, Eden realized they were airborne. Blue sky met her surprised gaze. She released the breath she forgot she held and watched the land fall away beneath them.

She was flying!

Eden wanted to laugh. She wanted to cry. She wanted to unhook her seatbelt and throw her arms around Jake's neck and . . . her heart stalled and fell to her feet as her stomach did a flip-flop. How could she even think about a Kipling that way? His family was responsible for the loss of her father. The bitter irony shrouded her happiness. Silently, she stared out the window, tuning out the conversation over the headset.

Eden had no idea how long they'd been in the air when she detected movement from the seat behind her. Turning her head, she saw Robert unbuckle his seatbelt and crawl into the back. Curiosity overruled her decision to remain quiet. "What's he doing?"

"I'm getting ready to winch the bird out so we can start our air mag survey." Robert's voice cackled over the headset as he sat down, his body obstructing her view of his task. Eden had noticed the computer screen and another box of what looked like electrical equipment when she boarded. Now she wished she'd paid attention.

Jake must have seen the puzzled look on her face because his voice broke into the temporary silence. "Remember this morning when I told you I was going to prove there is still copper in the mine?"

Eden nodded her head at his question.

"That's why we're here. We're going to drape a survey over Mina De Cobre to determine other possible structures related to the mine. Robert is going to lower the magnetometer attached underneath the plane so we can generate a contour map of the magnetic field. Once we've recorded our findings, we'll graph them onto a map, then do a ground follow-up."

All of a sudden, Eden felt sorry for him. He wanted so badly to believe copper existed that he'd almost had her believing it too. Except she accepted the old rumors as the truth; even her father had said many times at the dinner table that the ore grade was declining. All Eden needed to do was find the last surveys and prove there was very little left.

"You're wasting your time, Mr. Kipling. There's no more copper here. At least not enough to warrant reopening the mine."

"There is, Eden. I know it. I can feel it. But I'll promise you this, if you're right and the mine has been played out, not only will I leave you and Prosperity alone, I'll let you have the mansion, free and clear, for everything my family has put you through."

"We're at our location, Jake," the pilot announced.

"The bird's ready," Robert broke in before Eden could get a word out. Much as she'd like to dwell on the thought of her owning the mansion, her attention shifted back to the window.

They flew back and forth over the mine and outlying area, following a series of invisible lines. Eden didn't know how many times they passed by since she'd lost count, but with such a thorough survey, surely they would recognize the Mina de Cobre as a lost cause.

"Okay, we're all set," Robert announced over the headset. "Let me winch this thing in and we'll be on our way."

That was it? They were going back? After her initial sadness had dispelled, the sense of power and freedom she'd experienced left her wanting more. She wanted to fly with the birds all day.

"Bill, circle around to the east before we head back, I want to show Eden something." At a light tap on her shoulder, Eden turned and found herself nose to nose with Jake. She blinked in surprise. He leaned in so close that she could see the light dusting of freckles splashed across his face. Why hadn't she noticed them the other day? Funny how they made him look more human—more approachable.

If that was possible with a Kipling.

But that was beside the point. His nearness was doing funny things to her equilibrium. Or maybe it was the plane executing some kind of maneuver? She glanced at the pilot, but his hands were steady. Nope. The only movement came from Jake as he pulled the headset away from her ear and said discreetly, "If you look out my window on our next pass, Eden, you can see Prosperity just to the left."

"The entire town?"

"The entire town."

"Oh." Eden couldn't think of anything else to say. She'd always dreamed of seeing Prosperity from the air, soaring with birds though, not in an airplane. But it didn't matter. She fumbled with the latch of her seatbelt. Funny, she never had trouble with this type of belt before.

Jake made short work of the metal clasp, freeing her and helped her to her feet. She tried to ignore the jolt of energy that singed her entire being, but the current was too strong. Magnetic. Her gaze traveled to his face, his crystal-blue eyes. She lost herself in their depths, afraid, yet not afraid at the same time. The constant hum of the engines in her ears, the vibrations under her feet, ceased. Even the pilot and Robert seemed a distant memory. All that existed was the two of them—in one cramped space.

"Eden?"

She blinked. What was she thinking?

"Do you mind if I take your seat for a moment?" Eden had to sit down before her knees gave out, unsure if the sudden queasiness she felt was from his nearness or the altitude.

"Not at all."

Once she'd settled in his seat, the sensation in her stomach didn't cease. Jake had leaned in next to her, to where she could almost feel his breath against her cheek.

"Bank the plane a second, Bill."

As the Cessna rolled slightly, Eden concentrated on staring out the window. No one had ever gotten this close to her, gotten under her skin, under the protective layer that kept her from becoming involved with a man because she was afraid she'd lose him like she'd lost her father.

The realization stunned her. As did the fact that she was having these thoughts about a Kipling, no less. She shoved those thoughts away as the town appeared below her.

Eden had known Prosperity was small, just not how small. From the air, the houses and stores reminded her of little replicas of everything she knew so well. The few people on the streets were no bigger than her nephew's tiny green soldiers, the cars nothing but matchboxes.

As the plane veered away, she gave Prosperity one last look. Clinging to the brown hillside laced with scraggly trees, the town looked as if it were struggling to survive. And it was. As she was trying to do too.

But everything seemed so inconsequential when

looked at from this point of view. The only thing that remained a constant were the rocks and hills upon which Prosperity sat. They would be here long after Jake, Eden, and the town were long gone. That idea sobered her.

Jake studied Eden. Her face, filled with a kaleidoscope of emotions, left him wondering what she had been thinking since her smile had disappeared.

Earlier, her amazement at the simple things—things he took for granted—had taken his breath away. The sheer exhilaration written across her features, her gasp of pure astonishment, and the way she tentatively placed her hand on the window stirred the blood coursing through his veins. It still did.

He knew he could show her lots of things, take her to Europe or Australia if she wanted. He could bring her to New York and introduce her to his world . . . that idea almost made him choke. As his hand strayed to his ear, he forced it down to his side.

Eden's Spanish heritage combined with her small town charm and innocence wouldn't stand a chance against the prejudice of his white-bread friends. He sounded like a snob. Since when did he care what his 'circle' or anyone else thought? If they learned the truth about his own parentage, he'd be an outsider too.

He grimaced and motioned for the pilot to fly them back to Tucson.

Chapter Six

"Why does everyone assume I speak Spanish?" Eden questioned, shrugging her shoulders as the waiter walked away. Jake had insisted they stop for a bite to eat before heading back to Prosperity, and chose this quaint Mexican café close to the airport.

Starved since she'd gone without breakfast, Eden hadn't argued. She never turned down a free meal. Her passion for food, even though she carried around a few extra pounds, overruled everything else. Another hour in Jake's company at this point, since she'd already spent most of the morning with him, wasn't going to make much of a difference anyway.

"Don't you?"

"No! Well . . ." Eden suppressed a smile as she thought about her limited vocabulary. Her father had insisted they speak English around the house because her mother didn't speak Spanish. The two years of classes she'd taken in high school had long been forgotten because she'd never practiced.

Even her grandfather rarely spoke the language, except to a few old cronies, and the rare visitor that didn't speak English. Abuelo believed he should speak the language of his adopted country.

"Well what?"

She couldn't suppress her laughter. "I do know a few choice words, but Abuelo would have my hide if I ever used them."

"I'm afraid I don't understand, Eden. You—err have a Spanish last name, you look Hispanic, and your grandfather . . ." Jake quit speaking for a moment as the waiter dropped off their cups of coffee. "I assumed you would speak the language as well."

Pouring a huge dollop of cream and two packets of sugar into her mug, Eden used her knife to stir the light brown contents since the waiter had forgotten to leave a spoon. The soft clinking noise as the silverware hit the sides of the glass and the muted sounds of Latin music floating from hidden speakers were the only sounds in the room. Since the restaurant had just opened, they were the only patrons.

Jake looked decidedly uncomfortable when Eden glanced in his direction as she drank from her cup, so she chose to enlighten him. "I'm only a quarter Mexican. My grandmother on my father's side was Irish.

Grandma Louise, my mother's mother, always said that's where I got my pleasant temper." She grinned at her joke as she set down her coffee and grabbed a tortilla chip from the red plastic basket set in the middle of the table. She continued as she dug the homemade chip into the bowl filled with dark red salsa, "and my mother was half Italian, half Heinz 57. So in theory, Jake, I can curse you out in four languages."

Eden plopped the chip into her mouth and savored the tangy flavor. The salsa was good, but not as good as her grandfather's. She always judged a restaurant by the salsa. This one was okay, although the atmosphere was too sterile with its perfectly painted white walls and frilly blue curtains and tablecloths.

"Four languages, huh? That could be interesting." Unlike Eden, Jake only dabbed a bit of the hot salsa on his chip. The hot concoctions they produced down here were a little more than his palate could handle, though with time he was sure the flavor would grow on him.

Jake winced as the molten liquid burned the back of his throat. *Good Lord! How does Eden handle the stuff?* Hoping she wouldn't notice, he gulped some water from the heavy, hand-blown Mexican glass in front of him.

She did.

"You might try the other bowl. It's the mild stuff." Eden tapped a chip against the second ceramic bowl set next to the basket before she dug into the first one.

Forgetting the pain, Jake watched as she raised the chip to her lips and plopped it in her mouth. Between chews, she licked the hot concoction from her fingers. His discomfort arose again, but not at the back of his throat. He squirmed in the hard wooden chair.

"So, what about you? What kind of—what's the word—um—pedigree is Kipling?"

Jake knew she'd spoken because her lips moved, but he had no clue as to what she'd said. He hadn't heard her. All he could concentrate on was the tiny crumbs clinging so delicately to her lips and how he'd like to kiss them away.

"Jake? Hello? Do I have something on my face?"

Eden waved her hand in front of his eyes, snapping him from his hypnotic state. And not a moment too soon. "Sorry Eden. I didn't hear your question. Could you repeat it?"

Instead of answering right away, Eden reached for the last chip, then scooped up more salsa. She stared at it for a while, as if contemplating her next words. When she did speak, his reaction to her low, throaty voice made the salsa look mild in comparison.

"You know about my heritage, I was just curious to know about yours, that's all." She bit into the chip and used her other hand to catch the salsa that dripped off. Then, like before, instead of using her napkin, she used her tongue to lick it off.

Jake hid a groan by taking a sip of coffee. Mercifully, the waiter appeared with their food.

"Thanks. Could I get a little sour cream?" Flipping her ponytail over her shoulder, Eden gave the teenager a brilliant smile. As the waiter stumbled back into the kitchen, a puzzled look crossed her features. "Geez, what's his problem?"

"Maybe his shoelaces are too long?" Jake uttered the first thing that came to his mind. What made everything so enchanting was she had no idea of the effect she had on the opposite sex—including himself.

Her innocence and naivete brought out a different side of his protective streak. Thankfully, she was in the boonies of Arizona and not in some big city. They would eat her alive. Even his partner, Robert, had tried to put the moves on her at the airport this morning until Jake put a stop to it.

After the waiter dropped off the ramekin, Eden dug into her early lunch with gusto. "Mmmm. This is good. You don't know what you're missing, Jake."

Jake wished he knew.

He forced his attention to the plate in front of her heaped with rice and beans and one huge burrito, or burro, as they called it down here. She obviously enjoyed food, which was refreshing, since most of the women he knew would order a dry salad and leave most of it on the plate. But he'd already figured out that Eden was definitely not like anyone he'd ever met before.

Far from anyone he'd even remotely known.

She was a breath of fresh air to the stuffy, stuck-up

people back East. His mother's people. Eden represented his father's side. They were more down-to-earth, friendly, and gentle—he thought about Eden's earlier actions and grimaced—well, mostly gentle, though she had seemed to mellow some since their first meeting.

For the first time, Jake was beginning to feel like he belonged somewhere.

"Aren't you going to eat?" She looked at him over her burro, poised to take another bite.

In his preoccupation, Jake had forgotten his food. "Yeah, I'm just letting it cool a second. Don't let me stop you."

"Don't worry about that."

As she bit down, Jake had had enough. All morning long he'd wanted to find out what it would be like to kiss her. It took all his will power not to throw the table aside and grab her. He wanted to kiss her senseless. Maybe that would finally put an end to this crazy thing he was feeling.

But he wouldn't. Kiplings didn't do those things. Jake drained the rest of the water from his glass and signaled the waiter for a refill.

As she chewed, he noticed a miniscule amount of sour cream clinging to the corners of her mouth. Still, he longed to kiss it off, slowly, gently, teasing it away. . . .

"Is there something else wrong?" Eden questioned, looking at him speculatively. "You're still not eating."

"Uh—no." Nothing a cold shower couldn't take care of. His gaze fell to the container the waiter had left. He needed an excuse—fast. "Could I have some of your sour cream?"

"Sure. Finish it." Eden pushed the nearly empty ramekin toward him. "Abuelo tells me I eat too much of it anyway. He says I'll never . . ." Her voice dropped off and she turned to stare out the window.

"Your grandfather told you what?" Jake smeared the creamy mixture on his soft tortilla and folded the edges shut. He hoped the thing was edible, unlike the salsa.

A shadow crossed her features as the mid-morning sun edged its way through the open blinds. Eden sighed and turned to face him as she imitated her grandfather's accent. "Tsk, *Nieta*—you'll never get a man if you eat like that."

Jake doubted it. "That's nonsense." After considerable thought, her curvy figure appealed to him much more than the tall, willowy types he normally dated. He knew Eden would be soft and inviting in all the right places—but she was still definitely off limits, no matter how much he wanted to kiss her.

He bit down hard on his taco and chewed tentatively, not quite sure what to expect. The flavor surprised him. The moist chicken had been simmered with peppers, onions, and spices, then placed in a corn tortilla and topped with cheese, fresh lettuce, and tomatoes. Best of all, he could tolerate the mild heat from the peppers they'd used with the help of the sour cream.

"For once, you're right. That is nonsense."

Jake choked. He thought he'd never hear her utter those words, regardless that they had nothing to do with the mine. Was there hope after all?

"Are you okay?"

A look of concern sprang to her eyes as she leaned over to pat him on the back. He shrugged her off. He was afraid he might lose it if she touched him. His longing hadn't ebbed a bit.

"Fine. This taco is delicious."

"You had me scared there for a while, you know." Eden reached for another chip out of the second basket the waiter dropped off, loaded it with salsa, and popped it in her mouth. A mischievous look crossed her features. "You'll never survive here if you don't eat Mexican food."

"Is that an invitation?"

Eden shook her head. "Just a fact." She polished off the rest of her burro.

Jake dabbed the sauce that dripped from his taco with a paper napkin as Eden proceeded to lick her fingers again. Didn't the girl know how to use anything but her fingers? Without thinking, he started to lift his napkin to wipe her face, but stopped himself short and wiped an invisible spot of salsa on the tablecloth. He had no right to invade her space like that. This wasn't a date.

Jake dropped the napkin back on his lap and chomped on his taco and chewed like the devil was on his tail. Maybe he should reconsider opening the mine and make a beeline straight back to New York. But, like the woman sitting across from him, he'd made his own promises. He couldn't let Eden stand between them. No matter how sexy and desirable he found her.

Stopping to eat hadn't been such a great idea after all. All he could think about was Eden. Taking a swig of water to cool down his throat, Jake forced his mind to think of something else, anything else, to take his mind off of his current thoughts as he finished his meal.

"What was your mother's maiden name?"

"D'Amico." Eden cradled the coffee mug between her palms and eyed him over the rim.

"Your mother's maiden name was D'Amico?" Jake choked on his taco and felt his face go pale.

"Yes. Why?"

Jake looked down at the last few bites of food in his hands. No. Not D'Amico. Why did it have to be that name? Why couldn't it have been Smith or Jones or even Capone? After setting the taco down, Jake pushed his plate away, his appetite gone. Both Bart and Fred D'Amico were on the list of men killed at the mine. Not only had Eden lost her father, she'd lost two other family members as well. "Why didn't you tell me?"

"Tell you what, Jake?" After taking a sip from her coffee cup, Eden finally wiped the corners of her mouth with her napkin and gently placed it on the table. Her sigh spoke more to him than her actual words. "Would it have done any good? Would it have changed your mind?"

Jake didn't need to say a word since they both knew what the answer would be. He tossed a twenty on the table and pushed back his chair.

"Eden, can I talk to you a minute?" her sister-in-law asked as soon as Eden entered the diner. Eden didn't really want to talk to Lori right now, but since Lori had covered her shift, she felt obligated.

"Sure." After grabbing a steaming cup of coffee, she plopped herself down on the stool beside her sister-in-law.

"What's up?"

"It's about Jake Kipling."

Eden's hands froze as she tried to pour the cream. "What about him?"

"Some people don't think it's such a good idea for you to be going out with him."

"Going out with him? But it wasn't a date." Eden almost spilled her drink. Sure, maybe lunch might appear that way, considering the way Kipling looked at her while she munched on the chips and ate her burrito, but a date? No way. He was the opposition.

"Well, Mrs. Murphy thinks so. She was in this morning looking for you."

"Oh no." Eden groaned. She'd completely forgotten about her appointment with the postmaster's wife. They were supposed to discuss plans on how to attract other businesses into town. Not that Eden had spent a minute thinking about anything else but the mine and how to keep it closed.

"She asked me to tell you to stop by when you got home."

"Great." Cradling the ceramic mug, Eden drank the last of her coffee in one big gulp. She'd need the fortification of the caffeine to deal with what Mrs. Murphy would consider a misbehavior, even though Eden had nothing to hide. The older woman was one of Eden's biggest supporters. Without her influence and contacts, Prosperity would never attract the kind of business needed to survive. "Is there anything you need me to do before I go visit Mrs. Murphy?"

"No. I did everything while I waited for you to come back."

Eden stood. "Well then, thanks again, Lori. I guess I'll see you later. I need to get over to the museum for a while."

"Wait. There's something else." The borderline hysteria in Lori's voice made her stop. A shiver crawled up, then down her spine. When her sister-in-law made no effort to speak, Eden spoke up.

"What's wrong?"

"Adam begged me not to tell you, but I think you should hear from us first."

"Hear what?"

Eden sat back down on the stool. She could tell by the tone of her sister-in-law's voice she was not going to like what she had to say. The way Lori fidgeted with the salt and pepper shakers, juggling them around each other, confirmed her suspicion.

"Adam's going to put his name on the list to work at the mine."

"No!" Eden couldn't believe what she was hearing. "You can't be serious. The Delgados need to present a unified front. We'll find another way, we have to. There's no copper left, no matter what Kipling's surveys find."

"Eden—" Lori grabbed her hand and squeezed it gently. She looked as if she wanted to say something else, then thought better of it. But Eden didn't miss the hint of tears shimmering in her sister-in-law's eyes.

Taking a careful look at Lori, Eden realized that maybe things weren't going as well as she'd thought. Her sister-in-law's face appeared thinner than normal, and the bangs that fringed her face were cut unevenly, like Lori had trimmed them herself. Eden glanced at Lori's hands. For the first time in years, they weren't manicured and painted. Something wasn't right.

"Are you and Adam having money problems?"

"I—no." Lori gave her a smile that did little to reassure her.

"Then why is he doing this?"

"Because I want what's best for this town and my family." Lori pounded her fist on the Formica counter, startling her. Eden had never seen this side of her before. Lori was always so calm, so level-headed, so reasonable.

"What's best for this town and our family is for Kipling to go away."

Lori grabbed her purse and started to leave. "Is it, Eden?"

"Daddy, where are you?" Eden whimpered, jutting her arm into the thick blackness. Her hand met the cold, stony face of the boulder, blocking her escape to freedom. A sliver of light appeared yards above her head, illuminating her prison and the fine particles of dust kicked up by the fallen rock. She coughed and choked, unable to breathe or call to her father again.

Solid dark gray walls met an equally stark ceiling. The boulder in front of her was now embedded with shiny diamonds and other precious stones and twinkled in the filtered light. Behind her, the floor dropped off into nothingness. Yet across the wide expanse a door opened, spilling a white, hot light that barely penetrated the gloom.

A voice cut its way through the heavy atmosphere, surrounding her. Soothing her. "Eden? Where are you child?" Funny, it didn't sound like her father, but everything was distorted in the cave. "Help me, please."

Hearing desperation behind the words she turned, only to realize she lay flat on her stomach, trapped and powerless to use her legs. Fear paralyzed her rapidly beating heart. Unable to breathe, unable to speak, unable to move, Eden fought to retain a sense of control. She had to get out of here and she had to help whoever it was trapped inside with her—and quick.

The voice grew fainter with each second. She inched herself toward it, her fingers clawing the dirt beneath her, her legs dragging uselessly behind. She crawled on, gasping for whatever air she could pull into her burning lungs.

The abyss, dark and forbidding, yawned in front of her.

A hand clutched the rim—a large, white hand, not the callused brown hand of her father. Still, she reached for it, intending to pull the person to safety. Instead, the hand tugged at hers, ripping her away from the shelter of the ledge. She tumbled head first, falling deeper into the jaws of the earth.

The blackness swallowed her whole. Wind whisked by her ears and through her hair. A scream died on her lips. She could almost taste death as it reached up to meet her.

Suddenly, Jake's face hovered next to hers, his crooked smile giving her a sense of peace, his arms cradling her fall. Then he sprouted a pair of angel-like wings and lifted them both to safety.

Eden woke with a jolt. Drenched in sweat, she couldn't breath—or move. She could only lie there and clutch her pillow, trying to calm herself. The nightmare was back, made more realistic this time by the thin white sheet entangled around her legs and body, her head buried deep in her down pillow. But this time, instead of her father, Jake had appeared.

A soft click of a door shutting caught her attention. Eden slipped from bed and gazed out her window. In the stillness of the moonlit night, she saw Mrs. Jackson quietly walking down the alley, her purse slung over her shoulder.

Before she climbed back in bed, Eden glanced at the alarm clock to read the brightly-lit red numbers. Three-thirty. The only thought that crossed her mind as she drifted back to sleep was that Nana must have forgotten her medication at the diner and had come to pick it up.

Chapter Seven

"What's wrong?" Jake asked, stepping in beside the machine operator, Bud Rivers. The burly man, arms covered with more tattoos than Jake had seen in a lifetime, wore a perplexed expression.

"Someone's been messing with the front loader."

"How so?" At first glance, the heavy piece of equipment in front of them appeared normal, until Jake spotted the massive tires bulging slightly.

"Is it operational?"

"Naw. I don't think so. All the air's gone." Pulling on his bright red suspenders, Bud rolled back on the heels of his feet. The motion twisted Jake's gut into a tighter knot. "It don't look bad now, but once I lift the bucket and put the full weight of this baby on 'em to start blading—"

Jake swore under his breath.

"Why'd someone do this?" Bud scratched the scalp beneath his military-style crew cut, obviously left over from his days in the service.

Jake didn't know the answer, but he sure would find it.

At the sound of an approaching vehicle on the dirt road, he turned his head. Robert pulled up alongside them in his rented jeep. "What's going on?" he called to them, jumping from the cab.

"Vandalism. You'd better go to town and get the deputy sheriff on duty, Robert. Bud and I will stay here and make sure nothing else was damaged."

Robert whistled as he hopped back into the truck, slammed the door, and spun out, sending up a cloud of dust. Jake watched the machine operator squat down by the front tire and feel along the rubber surface. "No cuts or drill holes. All they did was let the air out. Good thing too, them tires cost a thousand bucks a piece to replace."

A small sense of relief coursed through him. A small act of mischief, just enough to put them behind a day or two. A day or two he didn't have. Jake kicked the deflated tire with the toe of his work boot. He didn't need any setbacks.

His network chart didn't allow for any delays, nor did his investors. The mine had to be running in less than nine months. Jake pounded the side of the yellow front loader in frustration before kicking the tire again.

They had to level the site today. The contracting company from Carter was due in tomorrow to pour the foundation for the new headframe.

"Does this town have a tire repair service that can come fill these things up?" Jake turned his attention back to Bud, who had just finished inspecting the hydraulic hoses on the side.

The operator shrugged his shoulders. "I dunno, Mr. Kipling. I live in Carter. I know there's one there."

Jake pulled out his cell phone and threw it to the man. "Call them. I don't care how much it costs. Tell them to get out here and take care of this now."

Since Bud Rivers knew more about the front loader than he did, Jake left it to the other man to make the call and check for more damage. With nothing to do now but wait for the deputy and the tire service from Carter to appear, Jake paced around, stopping where the level ground sloped off.

He made a mental note to hire security tonight instead of waiting for more equipment to arrive. Cutting such a minor expense, no matter how temporarily, had backfired. Distance and the thick, chain-link fence hadn't been a deterrence after all.

Settling down on the hard ground, Jake picked up a pebble and pitched it down the side of the hill at a scrawny tree about twenty yards off. He didn't know what kind of tree it was, nor did he particularly care as the rock struck the base, then landed harmlessly a foot away.

He scanned the rugged landscape. Dusty brown mountains turned into dusty brown valleys as far as he could see. Occasionally, a pale green tree or cactus dotted the nondescript backdrop, while the cloudless sky seemed to drift on forever. Complete isolation.

How different from what he was used to. Jake missed the lush greenery of upstate New York. And in a few weeks, he'd also miss the spectacular show of color as the trees changed to a sea of orange, yellow, and crimson. He inhaled deeply, trying to swallow the sadness. The hot, dry air stung the back of his throat and burned his lungs. Not even the slightest hint of a breeze. He missed his home town in upstate New York, even though he'd spent a lot of time in the Big Apple when he wasn't out in the field working.

Of course Eden would only be too happy if he returned there. But if he did that, he'd be denying not only his dream, but his heritage as well. Not to mention the fact that he had nothing to return to. Sure, his stepfather would take him in, but unless he changed professions, he had no job opportunities.

This was his last chance to prove himself. He'd made a mistake before. A monumental one. But this was different. He knew it in his blood. Copper still existed in this mine: he could feel it, breathe it, taste it. He just needed to prove it to those who doubted him—Eden included.

He knew he was doing the right thing for the town.

Jake picked up another rock, this one the size of a

small apple. He tossed it between his hands, the weight steadying him. This piece of earth remained a constant, the one solid thing amid the chaos that reigned around him. He squeezed a hand around the rock, allowing the rough edges to scrape against his fingers and palm before he set it down next to him instead of throwing it like he had the other. Neither the rock nor the tree had done anything to him.

But someone else had.

Jake racked his brain for an answer. Why had someone deliberately tampered with the front loader? And why only let the air out of the tires when more serious and time-consuming damage could be done? Who would hike from town to do this?

His gaze strayed toward Prosperity. The span wasn't that far—three miles from town, half a mile from the gate. Jake would ask Tyler McAllen, or whoever came to fill out the report, to look for tire marks near the gateposts. Someone in good health could walk the road in fifteen to twenty minutes.

A pair of sexy, muscular legs entered his mind. Eden.

He thought they'd come to some kind of truce yesterday, but obviously, it didn't last. Jake ran an agitated hand through his hair while her words from Saturday night echoed incessantly through his brain.

Accidents happen. The bitterness in her voice and the shadows in her eyes haunted him. Tearing up signs was one thing, tampering with equipment was something completely different.

"Open the door Eden, I know you're in there," Jake called out, rapping on the heavy wooden door of the museum again. He didn't want to pound on it for fear of drawing more unwanted attention to himself. Especially since the diner was right across the street.

The music blaring inside ceased, followed by the sound of the dead bolt sliding back. The door swung open, the damp coolness from the swamp cooler drew him inside.

"What do you want?" Her voice sounded odd today—the breathy, yet tired sound did things to his insides that he didn't like.

He edged his way past her and almost tripped over a mop handle hanging precariously along the rim of a bucket. Sudsy water spilled onto the freshly washed floor. The smell of pine assaulted his nostrils, underlined by the lemon scent of polish.

It took another minute for his eyes to adjust to the dim interior. That she'd been cleaning was an understatement. The place practically shone. The glass cases sparkled, the layers of dust lay at the bottom of a rickety old garbage can, and in the corner he saw a broom with a piece of old sheet attached so she could reach the cobwebs dangling from the ceiling.

He turned to face her, groaning when he saw her outfit of the day. Didn't the woman own anything decent? The red bandanna tied around her head covered more than the rest of her clothing combined. Her crimson T-shirt, similar to the one she'd worn at the cemetery, barely covered anything, and her shorts . . . Jake hoped she didn't bend over to pick something up or he wouldn't be liable for his actions. His determination to keep his distance was dying a somewhat painful death.

He shifted his attention from her scantily-clad body to her face. It was the gentlemanly thing to do, plus if he didn't he'd forget what it was that he came in for.

"Rough night last night?" he questioned, noticing the slight smudges beneath her eyes.

"No," she answered quickly, avoiding any eye contact with him, while her hands fidgeted with a string of cotton unraveling from her jean shorts. "What makes you think that?"

Her complexion paled and made the circles stand out even more. Jake's insides started to twist in agony at her physical reaction to his question. Actions spoke louder than words.

He had his answer.

So why couldn't the accusation leave his lips? Because he wanted to believe in her innocence. He wanted to believe her incapable of such vandalism. He wanted to believe in her, period. But what he wanted, and what she wanted, were two different things.

Only one of them would succeed and Jake knew it would be him. It had to be.

As he gazed at her face, something crawled in his line of vision. Jake shuddered. "Do you like spiders?"

"They're okay. Why? Where is it?"

He watched as she used her fingers to brush the fringe of her bangs. She amazed him. Most women would have started to scream and run around flailing their arms in terror. But not Eden. No. She stood there waiting for him to do something.

Except Jake hated spiders and anything with more than four legs. But as a Kipling he'd been taught, with the backside of Charles's cane, not to let anyone sense his fear—a ridiculous one at that—but one that could bring him to his knees if he allowed it. Inhaling a tad bit more than normal, he reached up and flicked the brown spider from its perch.

"I believe he wanted to make a home in your hair," he retorted, covering his anxiety with humor, before he permitted his fingers to extract the filmy web covered with dust.

Her hair was silky as he thought it would be. So was the skin on the tip of her nose as he brushed away a streak of dust that had settled there. As she squirmed under his scrutiny, her lips, parted in surprise, invited him to explore further. Except that wasn't why he was here.

Jake reached for one of her hands and lifted it for further inspection. Her fingers, tipped by healthy, short nails captured his attention. No dirt. Some of the tension trapped in his gut dissipated, until he remembered she'd been cleaning. Immersing her hands in the water for any period of time would remove any dirt that could have been stuck underneath.

He flipped her hand over and traced a figure eight onto the palm. No cuts or bruises, only a few calluses, softened by the cleaning water.

Could this tiny hand be the one that caused the damage at the mine last night?

Jake didn't know what to think anymore. So he didn't. He turned her hand back over and brought it to his lips. The lingering scent of fresh pine clung to her skin.

"So soft, so silky, what's your secret?" He wanted her. He wanted her so bad it hurt. But he couldn't have her. She stood between him and his dreams. Charles must be laughing in his crypt right now.

Eden yanked her hand out of his grasp and stepped back to regain some of her equilibrium. Whenever the man came within a foot, her mind went blank while her body went into overdrive. Why had she been cursed to be attracted to someone she despised?

She filled her lungs with much needed oxygen as she willed her heart to quit pounding so furiously in her chest. Seducing her hadn't been on his mind when he'd entered: she could tell that by the expression on his face and the rigid stance of his body. So what kind of game was he playing now? "What are you doing here, Jake? What do you want?"

Grabbing the mop, she wrung it out and quickly dabbed at the puddle Jake had spilled earlier. If she didn't do something with her hands, she'd probably throw her arms around his neck and beg him to kiss her. *Traitor.* Finished mopping, she continued to hold the wooden handle as much for support as a weapon if he should try to get any closer.

Jake paused for a second, passing a dirt-stained hand across his face. In the process he left a ruddy brown streak across the rough plane of his cheek. Eden suppressed the longing to clean the spot, like she'd cleaned every other object inside the museum today. Touching and being touched by Jake Kipling left her feeling out of her league.

"I came to see if you found the surveys yet."

Eden hesitated, amazed at how Jake could turn his emotions on and off like a switch—from angry to demanding, to warm and sensuous, to strictly professional. He must have a lot of experience. Experience Eden lacked. His infuriating presence made her feel inadequate.

Eden squared her shoulders, determined not to let him sense her shortcomings. "No. I got sort of sidetracked cleaning." Walking past him, she headed straight for the file cabinet where they'd already looked.

Maybe, just maybe, they'd miraculously reappeared.

The drawer squeaked when she pulled it open again, but with one quick look she knew the files were not there. She scratched at the back of her neck, as if that would give her the answer to the riddle.

"If the records aren't here, where do you think they might be?"

"I don't know."

Jake didn't like the answer. But somehow he knew Eden wasn't responsible for the records' disappearance. She'd have more to gain by showing them to him. Could it be that same someone who was behind all the disturbances?

"Who else has access to the museum?"

"Everyone. I leave the keys at the diner. Anyone can come in whenever they want, as long as the diner is open. All they have to do is ask for the key. But to my knowledge, nobody's asked to come in here outside of museum hours for years. Maybe Abuelo or Mrs. Jackson let them in."

"Are you sure the records really existed?" Jake hated to ask the question, but desperation made him do it.

"I know they did." The determination in her voice matched the glint in her eyes.

"What's in here?" He directed his thumb toward a closed door off to his left.

"The closet. I doubt they'd be in there since they were usually kept in the filing cabinet."

Jake opened the door and stuck his head inside. The

small closet contained a bunch of things, but nothing that resembled a box full of old surveys.

"What's this?" He pulled a wooden box from behind the huge stack of yellowed and dusty newspapers.

Recognizing the case, Eden felt the blood drain from her face. She crumpled to the floor, her legs unable to hold her weight. A searing shaft of pain coursed through her body as the memories bombarded her already sensitive nerves.

"Eden?"

"Don't touch that." She crawled forward and grabbed the box from his grasp. The smoothness of the pine wood top, which her father had painstakingly sanded and varnished while she watched, lay cradled in her arms.

"Go away." She hugged the box to her chest and rocked back and forth. Tears that had been held in for years spilled out from under her lashes and down her cheeks.

"What is it?"

"Go away. Leave—me—alone," she sniffled, the last word lost in a hiccup that racked her entire being. Using the palm of her hand, she swiped at the moisture, then wiped it on her shorts.

Swiveling around so her back faced Jake, she placed the box on the floor, rubbing her fingertips across the carved-out letters of her initials next to the latch. Life was so unfair.

"I didn't know you collect rocks."

"I don't."

But she did. Eden had a whole collection of pretty stones labeled and displayed in the wooden box her father had made for her. But she'd quit collecting the day her father died.

She lifted the lid. Inside, just as she'd left them, sat two dozen rocks, each labeled with a date, name and origin. The last entry on the day of the accident was the blue-green piece of Chrysicolla she'd found by the creek on the Kipling property.

Eden also remembered that she was to have gone into the mine that day for her birthday, instead of pretending like she did every day. There she could hunt for rocks herself with the pickax her father had bought her that last Christmas.

"Abuelo must have put the rock in there and hidden the box after—" Eden couldn't finish the sentence.

"After the accident." Jake did it for her.

Humiliated that she'd broken down in front of him, Eden slammed the lid shut, pushed the box underneath the desk, and whirled around, the hatred and bitterness fresh in her tears.

"Yes. After the accident. The accident that killed my father, my uncle, and my other grandfather. The accident caused by your grandfather." Her voice rose in volume and pitch until she didn't recognize it as her own. "I hate you, Jake Kipling. I hate you and your family and everything your name stands for."

She beat her fists against his chest as she sobbed

uncontrollably, her emotions out of check. Jake didn't flinch each time her hand struck his chest, even though she knew it had to hurt. But she didn't care. She wanted him to hurt, to know the pain, to feel as bad as she did. "Why did you have to come here and—and—I hate you." Tired, her pounding slowed as hiccups wracked her body.

Jake gathered her in his arms and rocked her gently as he rubbed the small of her back. To comfort her. That's all. "I'm sorry about what happened. I know words can't make up for anything, but please believe me. I'm sorry."

Somehow he wished he'd had a gentle pair of arms to comfort him when he'd learned the circumstances of his father's death. Nothing could ever make up for what had been lost to him either. On days like this, he really hated his grandfather, the name Kipling, and everything it stood for.

Despite the warning bells sounding in his brain, Jake leaned down and kissed her.

Chapter Eight

Eden didn't resist. She couldn't even if she'd wanted to. Kissing Jake Kipling was like eating Abuelo's homemade jalapeno salsa—mild at first until the heat kicked in, consuming her from the inside out.

She could easily become addicted to this.

With a sigh she melted into him, allowing his lips to caress the corners of her mouth. Gentle yet firm, they kissed her senseless, just as she thought they would. She'd been right in thinking he'd be like holding onto a big teddy bear. A living, breathing, warm teddy bear.

Her hands bunched up the front of his polo shirt and pulled him nearer and an anguished moan escaped as she kissed him back. She couldn't remember the last time she'd been so thoroughly satisfied. Her occasional dates left her wanting, wishing she'd opted to stay home with Abuelo, reading a good romance book.

But no. Not this time. Not with Jake Kipling.

The frigid thought doused the flames into a river of ice. This man who could ignite such incredible emotions was a Kipling, a murderer, and the only one who could erase the loneliness and grief in her life. Life was cruel.

She pushed herself out of his arms, fighting the urge to slap him. But how could she? She'd been as willing a party to the crime as he.

As she stared at a spot past his shoulder, she shifted her weight from one leg to the other. What should she do now? The silence stretching between the two of them was intolerable, though much more preferable than the kiss a few minutes ago. Or was it? She felt the color rise on her cheeks. What an infuriating man.

"Unless there's something else I can do for you, Jake, leave me alone. I'd like to finish cleaning this place before the next century." Faster than a dirt devil, Eden pushed him through the door.

For a moment Jake stood in the hot sunshine, still reeling from the contact. Her kisses had almost thrown him over the edge, where he could have easily repeated his mother's mistake. He'd had relationships with several women, but none had responded to him on that level. Where their kisses had been cold and calculated, hers had been pure and unrestrained.

Her lingering scent invaded his nostrils while her

honeyed kiss caressed his lips. He had to fight the urge to go after her and beg her to finish what they'd started. Except Kiplings didn't beg.

Eden was off limits to him anyway. So why did he feel like forgetting his obligations and chasing after her?

Jake must have taken her at her word because Eden hadn't seen him for a week. But that didn't mean she hadn't heard about him. His name rolled off the tongues of everyone who entered the diner.

"Did you hear Mr. Kipling's hired my Tommy as his right-hand man?" Mrs. Gentry asked, puffing up like a proud peacock. She looked like one too, dressed in that navy blue top with green polka dots, Eden thought wickedly as she dumped fresh coffee grounds into the filter.

"Oh, Edith," Mrs. Jackson declared as she set down the plate of cinnamon rolls in front of the four white-haired ladies sitting in the booth by the window. "Your Tommy's been telling you stories again. Mr. Kipling's only offered him a foreman's job." Eden suppressed a smile as she pushed the start button on the coffee machine.

But her smile turned to a frown as she thought of how even her own brother had applied. Eden needed to see him after her shift today and talk some sense into him. The mine was not the answer to the town's crisis. They would come up with a solution. They had to.

"My Daniel's told me Mr. Kipling volunteered to coach the boys' baseball league next spring *and* that he's offered to buy them new uniforms," Mrs. Connery piped in as she helped herself to a sweet roll.

How the woman stayed so slim amazed Eden as she walked by to clear the booth next to them. The other three, unfortunately, looked like the rolls they gobbled down.

Every week, like clockwork, Mrs. Connery, Mrs. Gentry, Mrs. Valdez, and Mrs. Auftenberg came in for Abuelo's rolls and coffee, and to catch up on the town gossip with Mrs. Jackson.

"Well, I heard that young man's going to fix up Thompson's old boarding house for all the single young men who'll be working for him." Mrs. Valdez sighed. "It's such a lovely place. Why, I met my Manny there—"

"Maybe my Louise will finally catch a man. Lord knows there aren't enough around here. Right, Eden? Mr. Kipling would be just grand, but I'd settle for anyone right now," Mrs. Auftenberg chattered.

"Your Louise can't catch pneumonia, Daisy," Mrs. Gentry cackled, helping herself to another roll.

"Maybe Eden's got her eye on Mr. Kipling herself." Mrs. Valdez caught her eye and winked.

"Not if he were the last man on earth." Eden picked up the bus tub and rested it on her hip, remembering the touch of Jake's mouth against hers. Crimson tainted her cheeks and her legs threatened to buckle underneath her, though she managed to move to the next table that needed to be cleared. Glad the ladies hadn't noticed her discomfort, she called over her shoulder, "You tell Louise she's more than welcome to him, Mrs. Auftenberg."

The four ladies tittered.

"Leave Eden alone, you old biddies." Mrs. Jackson pulled a chair from another table and sat down with them. "Now did you hear Susie Chung has gone and got herself pregnant? This is a good one. Eden, child, bring me some coffee, will you?"

After delivering the brew, Eden lugged the dirty dishes back to the dishwasher, sorted, and racked them before sending them through the machine. Once washed, she let them cool, before she stacked them and put them back where they belonged. Mercifully, the diner was empty by the time she'd finished.

Eden sank into the nearest barstool. Jake Kipling. His name was everywhere. Not even work was a sanctuary anymore. Men and women, young and old, merchant or laborer. It didn't matter. A tangible energy coursed through the town, threatening to carry away the inhabitants of Prosperity like the water from a flash flood carries dirt and debris in its wake.

The whole town had been lulled into false hopes and dreams. The county's appropriation of funds, backed by the approval of the town, to build a new bridge proved it.

Eden wanted to scream.

"Got a minute, Eden?" Tyler McAllen's voice startled her. She hadn't heard the bells jingle signaling his entrance. Pushing the salt and pepper shakers back where they belonged, she hesitated a second before turning to face him. At ten o'clock in the morning, she knew this wasn't a social visit.

"Sure, Ty, let's sit over here." Eden headed toward the first table where they could talk in peace, away from the prying ears of her grandfather. Hopefully this conversation would end before Mrs. Jackson got back from the grocery store. That they'd run out of syrup seemed like a godsend right now. Eden didn't need any more rumors flying through town.

She sat down, resting her arms on the table in front of her, barely able to keep her fingers from drumming the worn Formica. "What's up?"

Tyler looked uncomfortable. Decidedly uncommon for him. "There's been some more trouble at the mine."

"What kind of trouble?"

At first, Eden's heart stalled, thinking that Jake might be hurt. Until she figured she'd be the last person Ty would confide in. The way he studied her hands, as Jake did the week before, started the gnawing sensation in her stomach again. This whole issue was going to give her an ulcer.

"I shouldn't tell you, but you'd find out anyway. Someone torched the steel posts of the headframe—"

"And Jake thinks I'm responsible." She quickly drew her hands into tight fists, but let them remain on the table. She had nothing to hide. All she was guilty of was dreaming about the man.

And what dreams they were.

Feeling the heat rise on her cheeks again, Eden watched as Tyler removed his tan cap and ran a hand through his blond hair. A gesture she hadn't seen him do too much until Kipling came to town. Throwing Mr. Davis, the town drunk, in jail every Saturday or breaking up an occasional fight at the Dry Gulch Restaurant & Bar was all the sheriff's deputy usually dealt with. Riots and other such disturbances weren't common place in Prosperity.

"No. Not exactly. But he knows, as well as everyone else in town, that you're opposed to the mine reopening."

"So that automatically means I'm the prime suspect. I didn't do anything, Ty."

"Then how can you explain this?" He pulled her dirty, worn work glove out of the sack he carried. "It was found at the scene."

Eden's mouth gaped. A denial sprung to her lips, only to die as the comprehension sunk in. Someone wanted Jake to believe she was responsible. But who? She left her gloves, along with her other gardening tools, in a crate on the back porch. Anyone could have taken them.

"Fortunately, only minimal damage was done, so Kipling won't press charges." Tyler reached across the table and engulfed her fists between the palms of his hands, squeezing them reassuringly. "I'm here as your friend. Don't do anything else out of anger that you'll regret in the future. Not only for your family's sake, but for the town as well."

His words calmed her—a little. Sooner, rather than later, she was going to have to set Kipling straight that no matter how much she opposed him, she wasn't responsible for the ongoing vandalism. She'd do it today, but she needed to see Adam before her meeting with Mrs. Murphy and the others, and her promise to Abuelo came first.

Chicken! Yep. A number one, certified, Butterball chicken complete with the trimmings. Maybe a few more days would diminish her shortness of breath and trembling hands she experienced every time Jake came near. Then she could confront him and ease Tyler's conscience.

"I'm glad you're my friend, Ty. Diana's very lucky."

"Speaking of Di, her birthday's coming up soon. Any ideas what to get her for a present?"

"Well-l-l," Eden drew out the last syllable as she grinned mischievously at Ty, "last time we were in Bisbee, I saw her eyeing this scrappy little red thing made of satin and lace. I was going to get it for her as a shower gift if the two of you ever decide to tie the knot, but I'll allow you the honor. Just don't keep us waiting anymore. Okay?"

She couldn't help but laugh at the horrified expression on his face.

Jake paused outside of Delgado's Diner, glad he'd had the foresight to look through the window first. With their hands united, Eden and Tyler McAllen appeared to be having an intimate moment together. So much for his belief in the county legal system. Hopefully, McAllen would be able to persuade Eden to stop tampering at the mine.

Loneliness crept into his heart as he watched the adoration shining from her face, and the way she laughed with the deputy.

If only she would look at him like that.

Jake broke out in a cold sweat. He didn't know where the thought had come from, but he realized that somewhere between the ore samples and charts, Eden had woven her way into his heart. For the first time in his life, he began to understand his mother's actions.

The tantalizing odor of frying bacon wafted by his nose as an older woman, dressed similarly to Eden, opened the door and entered, carrying a small brown paper bag. His stomach protested, reminding him he hadn't eaten today. Like a lovesick fool, instead of leaving, he walked in.

The bells on the door jingled again, and Eden's breath caught in her throat when she saw *him* enter. Had Jake come to accuse her in person? Silently willing him to sit in the booth furthest from them, much to her dismay, he sat in the stool right by the cash register on the counter and in her station.

"We'd better get back to work. I'll see you around." Tyler placed his hat back on his head and slid out of the booth.

"Good-bye, Ty. Thanks."

"Kipling." As Tyler tapped his index finger to his hat, Eden could see the universal signal that as far as the Ty was concerned, everything was taken care of.

If only she could be so sure. How could she stop something she held no responsibility for? Or did she? She couldn't deny the fact that Tyler had found one of her work gloves at the site. But how had it gotten there? Was she sleepwalking again? For six months after the accident she'd developed that problem. But she'd never left the house before.

Somehow she didn't think it possible to walk three miles to the mine, much less drive, fire up a blowtorch, and proceed to cut apart the steel beams of the headframe without waking up. Though maybe that explained why she was so tired this morning.

Eden stood and slowly headed for the counter. For any other customer she would have picked up the pace, but not Jake. She toyed with the idea of letting Mrs. Jackson wait on him, but the other waitress was already in the middle of taking an order from the couple who'd walked in behind him. She'd look kind of foolish if she ignored him, especially with Abuelo giving her the 'don't dawdle all day' look.

"Coffee?"

"Yes, please." Jake turned over the white ceramic mug. "Do you have milk instead of cream?"

"Of course, whole or two percent?"

"Two percent will be fine."

The way Jake wrapped his hands around the mug reminded her of his gentle strength and how he'd caressed her last week. And how he touched her every night in her dreams. Eden bit her tongue to keep a groan from escaping.

"Here." She tossed the menu at him, turned abruptly around, and retrieved a stainless steel container for the milk on the way to the refrigeration unit on her right.

The blast of cool air felt good on her heated cheeks. If she could barely serve the man coffee, how was she going to manage an entire breakfast? Maybe she should suggest a carryout. "Don't be ridiculous," she muttered. "Treat him like any normal customer." But that's just the problem, her inner voice screamed back. He's not just any customer.

Her practical voice won out. A paying customer was a paying customer. She returned with the pitcher and set it down in front of him as she grabbed her order pad and pen from her apron pocket.

"What'll you have?" she questioned, glad her voice didn't reflect the turmoil going on inside her body.

"I can't decide. What would you recommend?"

"Well, that depends. Do you like a traditional breakfast? Or something a little—" Why, he was flirting with her! His wicked grin and bright eyes accelerated her heartbeat to another level. As she drank in the sight of him, from his wavy blond hair, to his incredibly blue eyes, to his scraped and callused hands, she couldn't resist the temptation. Her voice dropped as she continued, "—or something a little spicier?"

"Surprise me."

That would be her pleasure. She wrote the order down on the ticket, turned, and hung it on the wheel for Abuelo. "Order in," she called out, then turned to acknowledge the three people waiting by the entrance. "I'll be right there, folks."

Jake's gaze followed her as she rounded the corner and stepped out from behind the counter. He'd started the flirtation, but Eden had willingly joined in. She sure didn't act like McAllen's girlfriend. If Eden belonged to him, Jake would beat the lights out of anyone who looked at her like he did. Scum. But he kept looking.

She filled out her light blue uniform to perfection. Jake appreciated the way it hugged her hips and bottom. Tight, but not too tight as to be obscene or hinder her ability to move.

As she leaned over to take away the fourth place

setting, Jake almost lost it. The bottom of her dress rode up, exposing more leg than was humanly decent. He grabbed his coffee and took a huge swallow. Eden must make great tips, but Jake wondered if Tyler McAllen approved of the way she did it.

He sure didn't. He had half a mind to go pull that ratty old sweater, long forgotten, hanging on the coat rack in the corner and wrap it around her waist.

Movement from behind the counter caught his attention. Jake looked over and found himself staring into the wary eyes of Eden's grandfather. "Order up," the old man announced in his thick, Spanish accent, before turning away.

Jake cleaned up his thoughts as Eden returned to the counter.

"Watch your hands, plate's hot," Eden warned as she set the oversized dish down. Retrieving the hot pad, she placed it in her apron, opposite from her checks.

"What am I supposed to do with this?" Jake managed to mask his surprise under the guise of a question. The bubbly concoction of goo, over what closely resembled some sort of eggs next to a blob of brown, wasn't exactly what he'd been expecting.

"You can do what you want, but I suggest you eat it."

"I figured that. What's it called?"

"Migas. Scrambled eggs, peppers, melted cheese

with refried beans, and tortillas on the side. Let me get you setup."

Eden grabbed three jars from the small cooler directly behind her where the salsa and jellies were stored and set them down next to Jake's plate. "Abuelo's homemade salsa. This one is mild." She pointed to the jar filled with chunky red tomatoes, peppers, onions, and cilantro. "This one is medium." She shifted his attention to the jar filled with green puree. "And this," she took a spoon from the place setting next to him and stuck it in, taking a small bit out and slowly licked it off with her tongue, "is Abuelo's *diablo agua*."

The last jar was only filled halfway with a dark red puree. Not many people had the stomach for her grandfather's famous, flaming-hot habanero concoction. She'd developed a tolerance for it because she grew up on the stuff.

The salsa burned on the way down. But it was mild compared to the looks Jake had given her earlier. She still tingled from head to toe.

"Oh really." Jake must have forgotten his experience with salsa in Tucson, because he took the spoon out and dropped a large dollop on top of the eggs in front of him. Before Eden could warn him, he cut off a section and placed it in his mouth.

"Jake, no!"

Too late.

Eden ran to get a glass full of milk to deaden the

sensation as she saw his face turn beet-red and his eyes tear up. He coughed and choked at the same time.

"What are you trying to do to me, kill me?"

"No. Quick. Drink this."

As Jake downed the liquid in two seconds flat, Eden sagged against the counter. Hard as she tried, she couldn't suppress the laughter building in her throat. She bit down on her lip but it didn't help, the giggle slipped out with her words. "Jake, I'm so sorry. I thought you knew—you weren't supposed to do that."

"You got me on that one." He wiped the tears as his rich laughter mingled with her own. "I'm going to live, aren't I?"

"Of course. I imagine it would take more than Abuelo's salsa to bring down a Kipling. You missed a spot." She grabbed the napkin from his grasp and dabbed at his cheek.

The intimate gesture stalled her breathing as well as her ability to move her hand away. Her fingers longed to run through his hair, massage away the lingering affects of her joke. Jake must have sensed her indecision, for he reached up and entwined his fingers through hers before dragging them down to his lips and kissed the back of her hand. "Haven't you figured out yet that nothing will bring down a Kipling?"

Chapter Nine

"I hear you've applied at the mine, Adam. How could you?" Eden questioned as she followed her older brother and watched him grab a soda from his refrigerator. Even though the interior light didn't work, she could see how empty the shelves were.

"I have no choice. I have a wife and two children to think about."

Adam sat down at the shabby kitchen table, shoving aside a stack of what looked like bills. Eden had never seen her brother look so worn—so beaten. She reached out and touched his arm. They had always been close, the bond forming after the accident, yet today her brother seemed distant, almost unapproachable.

Adam was silent for a moment as he took a drink from his soda. "Take a good look around. What do you see?"

A quick appraisal of the room left her feeling disjointed. The counters were cluttered with dirty dishes and empty boxes, the floor covered with a slight layer of dirt. An air of neglect pervaded the small room.

"What's happened, Adam?"

His shoulders sagged as he rubbed his hands over his face. "I lost my job weeks ago. I can't find another and the bills are piling up. Lori's taken the kids to stay with her parents in Tucson and has gotten a job there to help out for the time being. There. Are you happy now?"

"What? Lori's taken the kids away? She has a job? Why didn't you tell us?" Eden said as she rushed to her brother's side and gave him a hug. That explained why she hadn't seen them in town the past few days. "Abuelo and I could have helped you. We could've figured something out."

"That's exactly why I didn't tell you. I'm a grown man, able to make my own decisions." Adam pounded his fist on the table, upsetting the can of soda and Eden. She jumped and released her hold. "And like my father, I'm going to work in the mines."

"What if there's another accident, Adam? What would Lori and the kids do if something happened to you? Do you want Matthew and Maggie to grow up without a father like we did?" Eden couldn't keep the edge from her voice. How could her brother even take that chance?

"Grow up, Eden." Adam's voice lashed out at her.

"Our father knew the risks every time he put on his gear. Lori understands them too and backs me a hundred percent. We're counting the days until the mine opens and I can support my family again!"

"You're willing to take those same risks?"

For the first time in her life, Adam propelled her toward the front of the house. "I have to do what I have to do. Now get out before I say something I'll really regret."

Eden stumbled through the door. Her own brother had turned on her. How could everyone be so blind? Couldn't they see the truth?

What truth? She grabbed the lamppost just past Adam's property line to keep her legs from collapsing under her. The truth hit her square in her stubborn head. Jake Kipling had brought back hope to the people of Prosperity.

A false hope, in her mind, but hope nonetheless.

Eden sat staring into mid-air long after Mrs. Murphy, Mr. Rodriguez, and Mr. Gregory left the diner. Their third meeting to explore ideas on how to attract other business to town had failed again. They couldn't come to a consensus about which type of industry to vie for, nor what they could offer with their limited resources.

"I still think we could make this an artist community and build a tourist business." Eden ground her teeth in frustration.

"But in order to do that, we need to give the town

a facelift and that costs money," Diana answered glumly from the next seat. "Money the town doesn't have . . . but Jake Kipling does. What a mess."

Eden sprung to her feet and paced, unable to remain seated any longer. Jake had promised to donate funds for some of the restorations once the mine began producing copper. Which would never happen! "Money the town isn't ever going to have either. The mine has been worked out. Doesn't anyone remember the old surveys?"

"No. The other people who'd seen them are . . . gone now. You're the only one."

Eden stopped pacing and watched as Diana's gaze slid from the mug in front of her to her own.

"Did you ever find them?"

Eden shook her head. A sinking feeling settled in her stomach as she noticed the uncertain expression written across her friend's face.

"Maybe the person who took the records is also the person who's been vandalizing the mine." Diana spoke so softly Eden could barely hear her.

"Not you too. You don't honestly think I'm responsible for that—"

"Eden—I—I don't know what to think anymore. All I know is this town needs something. Maybe you should give Jake Kipling and the mine a chance."

For a moment, all Eden could do was stare at her friend. For the first time in her life, Diana seemed like a complete stranger. Had everyone gone mad?

"No. That's easy for you to say, your parents are still alive. The Kiplings didn't destroy your life like they did mine."

Silence shrouded the thickening atmosphere.

"You're right Eden, they didn't." Her friend slipped out from behind the table and walked stiffly to the back entrance. "But I'm not sure they're responsible for *all* the destruction in your life either. I'll see you around."

"Diana, wait—I'm sorry." Eden winced at the memory of the hurt that flashed through Diana's eyes. She felt terrible saying those things to her friend. Jake didn't even need to be present anymore for him to bring out the worst in her. Eden stared at the doorway long after Diana had disappeared.

Weary, Eden sank down onto the closest bar stool and folded her arms on the counter. "There has to be another way!" she whispered as she lay down her head and closed her eyes.

From where it lay, overlooked in a dim corner of the storage shed, Eden pulled the old pick from beneath an inch of accumulated Arizona dust. The metal, warm to the touch and rusted from years of neglect, stained the palm of her hand. What remained of the black leather on the handle slithered away like a lazy snake on a hot August day.

"Did you find it?"

Unaware of Jake's presence, Eden jumped at the question, cracking her head against a wooden beam.

Another layer of dust rained down, covering her freshly washed ponytail. Her sneeze sent another round of grime floating through the hot, stale air.

"Find what?"

"Whatever you were looking for."

"Excuse me." Eden backed out, still holding the toy pick in her grasp. Built for storage, not for human occupation, the shed barely fit her body. She didn't need Jake taking up any more room.

"What's this?" Jake reached for the metal object. She relinquished it, knowing it would be useless to stop him. He scrutinized it with an experienced eye before cradling it in his palm. At its widest point, the ax barely spanned the width of his hand. "An old toy?"

"Hardly." Eden brushed her hands together to remove the loitering dust. She turned to head toward the back door, only to be stopped by the gentle pressure of Jake's hand.

"Eden? Talk to me."

She made a beeline for the huge mesquite tree shading the back porch steps. Sitting on the hard wood, she patted for Jake to sit next to her. What did she have to lose? Fighting hadn't worked. Nor had anger. Perhaps a little more sympathy might make him change his mind.

If that didn't work, maybe she'd try a little friendly persuasion.

"This ax was my escape to freedom." She reached over and took it from him and gazed intently at the orange rust. Suddenly she was eight again, full of hope and dreams and exciting plans for the future.

Thunk. She banged the spike against the step, the pressure reverberating up and down her arm. A small chunk of metal flew, grazing the skin of her arm.

The family dog jumped from his perch next to her and, with his tail between his legs, slunk off to lie under the mesquite tree. "Sorry, Lucky." Eden grimaced as the old dog acknowledged her with a drawn-out groan. "Poor thing's so old and deaf I'm surprised he heard anything at all."

"I don't think his hearing had anything to do with the fact that he thought his doghood might be threatened." Jake shifted on the hard, wood step next to her. The way she flung that rusted ax around, he became a bit concerned for his well-being too and considered joining Lucky beneath the tree.

"Oh."

Much to Jake's relief, Eden quit pounding the ax on the wood. At least the porch would survive another day. Jake wasn't so sure about himself.

Her whole demeanor had changed. And he wasn't sure he liked it. He liked the fight and the spunk in her. It kept him on his toes and an arms length away from her. This friendly attitude, her willingness to talk to him, scared him. He might want to get used to it. Which of course was impossible, but he followed her lead. "Freedom?"

"I was the ice princess. Everything I touched would turn to diamonds and gold and other glittery stones."

Jake didn't have a hard time picturing her as a child, wearing a loose white dress, flowers entwined in her braids, as she leapt from rock to rock, leaving a trail of jewels in her wake. He could almost see the diamonds himself.

"What happened?"

"What do you think happened?" She turned to look at him, her chocolate-brown eyes gazed into his, the unshed tears tugged at his heart.

Jake didn't need to answer as he tasted the bile rising in his throat. How he hated the old man sometimes. He wondered if Charles ever really understood the suffering he'd caused these people. Why hadn't the old man paid more attention to the safety conditions?

His mind was turning to mush. He couldn't let the past ride up and overwhelm his desires. There had to be a solution that everyone could live with or he'd probably lose more in the bargain than just his sanity.

"I've got the results back from the air survey, Eden. I thought you might be interested in looking at them." Jake pushed himself from the step and stood. "When you're finished here, stop by the surveyor's building and I'll show them to you."

"Oh, I'm done. I just hadn't been in here for years. I was just looking around. I've had enough dust and grime for one afternoon." Eden stood and tried to brush as much dirt from herself as possible, but only succeeded in smearing it into her brightly colored tank top.

She groaned, wondering where she was going to get a clean outfit since she hadn't done laundry yet. That had been on the top of her list of chores for today, but as usual she'd procrastinated and now didn't have anything else to put on. Well, she'd just have to find something. "Let me get another shirt and I'll be right with you."

"You don't have to change for me, Eden. You look fine. Except for the smudge on your left cheek, you look no worse than I do."

Jake gave her an amused look that somehow didn't annoy her as it had done in the past. Forgoing a trip upstairs to change, Eden used the tips of her fingers to brush away the dirt that Jake had indicated too, though she knew she'd probably just made it worse.

This time she accompanied him to the surveyor's office willingly. The blood rushed to her cheeks as she remembered the other time she'd been here. Almost every day she ran into someone who'd witnessed her actions, though probably in deference to her grandfather, no one said a word.

Climbing the stairs under her own power, she noticed that the weathered boards had been replaced, as well as several planks on the porch. A new deadbolt shone on the original door as Jake unlocked and let them inside.

A fresh coat of paint had been added—a cream color—to match the blinds hung in the window, right over an air conditioning unit. A computer sat on the new desk, and the rickety old furniture had been replaced by its more modern equivalent.

Along the back wall, a freestanding bookshelf filled with an assortment of books grabbed her attention. Her fingers longed to reach out and touch them, just as she'd wanted to do when they were in the tower at the mansion.

"It looks nice in here, Jake." Eden had to say something to break the silence between them.

"Thanks. It's starting to look like an office now, isn't it?"

Eden nodded her agreement as Jake paced to the desk. She followed. "So what is it you wanted to show me?"

"This." What looked like a colorful computer-generated map lay on the desk. "See this anomaly here?" Jake pointed to a section of the map where a point of red shot out from the blue section. "This is interesting because it shows a variation. Something we should definitely focus on."

His excitement was contagious. Eden felt a rush of adrenaline as she traced the contours of the point. She'd never seen a map like this before, but the differentiation in the colors did strike her.

As her hand swept across the surface again, a tangible energy seemed to leap from the page. Was this truly a sign that there was copper in the mine? Had the old surveys been wrong?

"What will you do now?"

"Our next move is to do a ground survey of this location. Sorry Eden, but it looks as if I'm staying."

Her heart raced at the thought that Jake wouldn't be leaving any time soon. Somehow she'd become accustomed to his presence in town.

Could the old rumors have been just rumors after all? Had her father and the others been wrong? Nothing made sense anymore. Not this piece of paper, not the papers that she couldn't find, nor her response to the man standing beside her.

In order to make sense of this chaos raging inside her, she needed to feel the earth, feel this section Jake spoke about, not on some paper but the real thing. Maybe then her world would tilt back in line.

"Show me." Eden took a deep breath and wondered if she was losing it. What she had suggested meant spending more time with him—a dangerous proposition in her state of mind.

"Show you what?"

"You just said your next move is to do a ground survey. Take me with you and let me see for myself if this so-called copper still exists."

"But—"

"But nothing, Jake. I would've thought you'd jump at the chance to prove me wrong." Eden walked away and looked out the window, staring at the dusty street and run-down town around her. Swallowing her pride, she turned and looked back at Jake. "Remember what you told me at the mansion, Jake? You asked if I would stop fighting you if you could prove there was copper in the mine. Well, Jake. Here's your chance. Show me."

Jake didn't need a third invitation. After grabbing the black box containing the portable magnetometer from underneath the desk, he retrieved his keys and headed toward the door. "Let's go. We've only got a few hours before the sun sets. Let's see what we can find."

Silence prevailed in the Navigator as they drove out of town. Jake didn't dare say a word to break the almost companionable atmosphere between them.

After retrieving the magnetometer from the back seat, Jake locked his vehicle. He shouldn't have to, but with all the trouble still happening at the mine, he had no choice, even though the person who he suspected was behind it all stood only two feet away from him. He just couldn't prove it.

As his gaze raked over her again, he still found it hard to believe that Eden would do the destructive things that were happening; tearing down his signs and passionate speaking were more her style.

A slight breeze stirred the stillness, bringing with it a hint of fall in the air. The temperature had cooled slightly, but it was still hot compared to the weather he was used to. Homesickness tugged at his heart until he realized he had nothing to go home for. His life was here now. For better or worse.

The only sounds they heard as they trudged over the rugged terrain were the cawing of a black crow and the crunch of the earth beneath their feet. The same held true even when they got to the location Jake had seen the anomaly on the survey. The magnetometer was silent.

He began to pace with an urgency, his long strides no match for Eden. "It has to be here somewhere. It has to," he muttered. But the longer the contraption in his hands remained silent, the more anxiety ate at his insides. His investors were going to want answers soon, and so far Jake had nothing but a dry claim and unforeseen bills due to the vandalism.

"Jake, why is it so important for you to find copper here?" Eden questioned as she finally caught up with him, her hand stopping him mid-stride.

She motioned him to join her as she sat down on the warm rock and gazed out over the harsh landscape. One that she loved, not knowing anything else. How different it must seem to someone from upstate New York, where according to the books and movies the landscape was green.

Yet somehow Jake fit in here.

Eden shivered. The sun started sinking over the mountain, casting a shadow over them. Soft fuchsia fingers stretched toward them from the east, chased by the darkening color of night.

Jake joined her, edging himself close because the rock outcrop could barely accommodate him, much less both of them. Eden squirmed but didn't move. She wouldn't let Jake know of her discomfort. His kiss at the museum the other day still rattled her composure.

Still, she longed to reach out and caress the lines of worry that had formed around his eyes.

"You wouldn't believe me if I told you."

"Try me."

Jake picked up a small rock and threw it. "I made a huge mistake at the last company I worked for. I misinterpreted some vital information that cost the company millions of dollars."

Eden saw intense bitterness flit across his features before a mask of indifference settled upon him. The thought struck a chord with her. She struggled to keep her hands at her sides. She hated the man and everything he stood for. Or did she?

"Someone intentionally seeded the ore samples to make it look like there was more ore in the mine than there actually was. Of course, the situation wasn't discovered until the company started mining operations."

"But how can you blame yourself?"

"I'm a professional. I should have seen it. Everything was wrong. The lay of the land, the other surveyor. Do you know his uncle owned the land? They made a fortune. If we'd looked closely enough, we would have seen it."

"Aren't you afraid of making the same mistake here?"

"No!" Jake jumped to his feet. "This is different. I can feel it. We're not looking in the right area."

Eden picked up a handful of dirt and examined it closely. The light brown gravel glistened with color, intensified by the setting sun. Her life, her blood, was entwined with the very earth that she now let sift through her fingers.

And suddenly she knew. She could also feel it. There was copper here. Somewhere.

After brushing her hands free, she rose slowly. "You're right. It's here. You're looking in the wrong place. Have you tried below the surface?"

He gave her an incredulous look. "Did you say what I think you just said? You admit that there is copper here?"

Begrudgingly, she gave him a slight smile as she began to trudge back to the car. "Don't push your luck. I admit there is copper here, okay, but there was still copper here before the mine shut down. I'm not certain how much is actually left."

What she didn't tell him was that she was starting to believe that the old surveys were wrong. That she was starting to believe in him. And that idea scared her to pieces.

"I need to get back before Abuelo starts to worry."

He kept pace with her, his voice regaining the confidence she'd come to associate with him. "Maybe you're right. I'm not looking deep enough. Robert and I are going in the mine tomorrow at noon. Care to join us?"

Chapter Ten

Jake cursed under his breath again as he glanced at his watch. It was almost time to get ready to go into the mine, but instead of taking care of the things he needed to get done, he'd been preoccupied with other things.

Someone had vandalized some of the new equipment last night, and he'd spent the entire morning with Robert trying to figure out how to put it back together again.

The night watchman, whom he'd hired after the first incident of trouble, had neither seen nor heard anything. When he'd patrolled at two A.M., everything had been fine. When he made the rounds at three, the tires had been slashed and the wires pulled from the top loader engine.

Jake walked around the scene, barely able to distinguish any marks in the hard, dry ground. Every once in a while he caught a glimpse of a print of a badly worn tread from what looked like a bicycle tire.

His thoughts returned to Eden. The damage done previously were things she was physically capable of doing. Nothing that really required brute strength or force. But again, after yesterday, he'd thought they'd come to a truce. Especially after she admitted her feelings that there too was copper in the mine.

He kicked the dirt with his heel, then wandered back into the mining office, wondering if Eden would dare show up today, and what his reaction would be if she did.

"That's funny." Eden jumped off her bike and lowered the seat as she spoke to Lucky. "I wonder who rode this last? Adam must have borrowed it." Lying on the back porch, her dog thumped his tail enthusiastically, but didn't lift his head to acknowledge her words.

"Oh you." She leaned down to pat Lucky. "I'm going to the mine, want to go?" He lifted his head, rolled his eyes, and exhaled loudly as his head thumped back on the wooden porch.

Eden took off down the alley, turned right on First, then another right on Main, and headed out of town. At the mile turnoff, she paused to collect her wits. With the exception of yesterday, she hadn't been on the winding dirt road that led to the mine since the day of the accident. There'd been no reason to be, until now.

Jake had invited her to go into the mine, and it was an opportunity she couldn't pass up. Once inside, maybe she could finally put those feelings that copper still existed to rest. For better or worse.

Her hands shook as she wiped them against her jeans, grabbed the curved handles, and forced her feet onto the pedals. The two miles passed quickly.

At the barricade, she pulled off her cap and wiped the sweat from her brow, then took a swig of cold water from her bottle.

New foundations had been poured, securing two shiny new posts, a double section of one-inch looped chains strung between them. This would keep unwanted vehicles out, but not Eden. She dismounted and pushed her bike around the posts, then rode the rest of the way to the mine.

The site was empty. Above her, two hawks soared, reminding her of her dreams of flying and how Jake had made them a reality. Just as he was making the mine a reality and bringing hope to the people of Prosperity.

But she wasn't totally convinced . . . yet.

"Good afternoon, Eden. Back to make more mischief?"

Still gripping the handlebars, Eden whirled around

to face Jake. "Of course not. Why? Did something happen?"

She scanned the area again, but didn't see anything wrong or out of place.

"What do you think?" Jake wiped his forehead with the back of his sleeve. Perspiration soaked his collar and stained circles underneath his arms.

Not knowing what else to say, Eden apologized. "Jake, I'm sorry. How bad is it?"

"Bad enough to set us back a few days."

He gave her a hard look that sent a shiver down her spine, but he was blaming the wrong person.

"No matter what you think, or how you feel, I didn't do it. Sure I've opposed you all along, but all I'm guilty of is tearing down your signs and inciting riots. Please believe me."

Her choice of words brought a smile to his lips and softened his expression.

"I don't know why I do, but I believe you, crazy as it seems. Now if you want to go into the mine sometime today, we'd better go get ready. Robert's probably pacing by the office door by now."

"Hello Eden, good to see you again. Jake, Donald Parker's ready to send us down whenever you are," Robert said as soon as they entered.

"We'll be ready in no time," Jake replied.

As Eden reached behind him and grabbed a hard hat from the peg, Jake took a yellow slicker from the next peg and handed it to her.

"Put this on too. It may be a hundred degrees up here, but down there it'll be about fifty." He took two more slickers from the coat rack, threw one to Robert, then donned one himself.

"Here's a battery pack," Robert said, handing Eden a leather belt with a small battery attached to the back. "Do you need help putting it on?" His quick smile put her at ease until she glanced in Jake's direction. His scowl disarmed her. She fumbled with the catch and the belt clattered to the floor.

"Careful, Eden. It's awfully dark down there if you don't have a light," Jake said. He halted in front of her and picked up the belt. "Raise your arms."

She grasped for the belt, but Jake held it just out of her reach. "I don't need any help. I watched my father put one of these on many times."

"And I'm sure your father was a capable man, but we don't have all day. Now raise your arms."

His sudden shift to a sour attitude surprised and disarmed her, but Eden obeyed. She lifted her arms just enough so Jake could wrap the belt around her waist and cinch it tight. Then he plugged in the cord that had a small light attached on the end.

"It's easiest if you run this over your shoulder like this." Jake eased the cord from behind her back, ran it up the left side of her body, then under her ponytail and around her neck. Eden quit breathing as his hand lingered a second longer than necessary as he laid her hair back in place and dropped the unit into her palm.

"Now what?"

Jake stepped back and attached his light to his hat with such ease that Eden had no doubt he had a lot of experience—and some of it had nothing to do with mining at all.

"You can either hold the light in your hand or attach it to your hat like I did. I'd suggest you put it on your hat so you have your hands free. All set, Robert?"

"Just about." Eden watched as Robert strode over to grab another battery pack hanging from the wall. "You can never have too many of these with you," he replied to her questioning look as he slipped the unit into his pocket, cocked his eyebrow, and gave her a mock bow. "After you."

"Why, thank you, Robert." Eden grinned at his boyish behavior. She couldn't help but like him. "At least someone has manners around here." She stole a glance at Jake as Robert threaded his arm through hers. His sour expression deepened.

"I have manners alright," Jake replied through clenched teeth as he advanced and took hold of her other arm. He didn't know what kind of game his partner was playing, but he had to put a stop to it now. "Allow me."

Even through the yellow slicker Jake was aware of her. This was going to be a long afternoon if the mere touch and scent of her drove him beyond rational thought. If he had any sensible brain cells left, that is.

Suddenly, Jake wanted to kiss her silly. Despite

everything, this loyal, passionate woman who loved food and wasn't afraid of spiders had gotten under his skin.

"Let's go." Jake escorted her to the entrance while Robert paced beside them. "Ladies first."

The cage, which looked like an elevator with no sides—just metal bars with a floor and a ceiling—could hold several grown men at a time, gear and all, and looked no different than the one that used to take her father and the others below the surface.

"Where are we going?" Eden questioned as she stepped into the contraption. It swayed slightly from the motion, but not enough to concern her.

"Level five. We'll start there and work our way up." Once inside, Jake snapped his switch. "It's time to turn your light on."

Eden did the same and so did Robert as the steel gates slammed shut, the loud thud echoing in Eden's ears. Anticipation replaced any apprehension that gnawed at her insides. This was what she'd always wanted.

Jake signaled the hoistman to lower them into the shaft. The downward motion startled her at first, as did the inky darkness once they were away from the entrance. Her gaze fixated on the solid wall of rock in front of her, her eyes adjusting slowly to the light thrown from her lamp.

Eden was glad for the slicker. Jake was right, the temperature had dropped quite a few degrees since they'd left the surface. The dank smell of wet rock invaded her nostrils as her fingernails bit into her palms.

The darkness was overwhelming.

"A penny for your thoughts?" Jake wrapped an arm around her and settled her against him. "You're awfully quiet."

Eden sank into him, relieved. Her father had never prepared her for the reality of the mine. He'd always made it sound so exciting, so beautiful, so exotic. "It's not what I expected." No matter how hard she tried, she couldn't keep the disappointment out of her voice.

"It's not?" Jake gave her a squeeze. "That's because the adventure hasn't begun yet. Sometimes the things really worth having take a long time to get. But it's the time that it takes to get the thing that is really the—"

The cage jolted to a halt.

"What's going on, Parker?" Jake yelled to the hoistman.

"What's happening?" Eden questioned, grabbing his arm to stop herself from falling. "Why are we stopping?"

Robert shifted uneasily. "Looks like we're stuck."

Both Robert and Jake looked at Eden.

"What are you looking at me for?" She returned Robert's gaze first, then Jake's. Her heart dropped to her knees. The condemnation written in their eyes sent a shiver down her spine that had nothing to do with the cool temperatures. She stepped back until the hard metal of the rear of the cage stopped her.

"I told you earlier that I didn't have anything to do with the vandalism, or this. I swear it, Jake. I may be opposed to you reopening the mine, but I'm not the only one."

"Then give me some names of who could be."

Eden couldn't think of a single person capable of doing such destruction. The other opposition members were either women, or too old. So naturally, she was the logical culprit. Or someone wanted Jake to think so.

Silence lingered, until Robert's voice cut through the dim atmosphere.

"She's right, you know. There could be a logical explanation that has nothing to do with what's been happening."

Jake passed a quick hand over his face, then let out a sigh as he let his arm drop to his side. "We won't know until we get to the surface."

"Well, what do we do now?" Her voice sounded small, insignificant in the dark recess of the mine.

"Looks like we're going to have to climb out," Robert answered her. With that he pried the top of the cage open, and with the help of Jake, pulled himself through. "Give me your hand." Robert reached down and grabbed Eden by the wrist as Jake lifted her by the waist. Once on top of the cage, Eden and Robert moved off to the side to allow Jake to hoist himself up.

"Where are we?"

"My guess is somewhere between levels four and three," Jake answered her as he tugged at the metal ladder attached to the shaft wall. "Feels secure to me. You go first, Robert, then you, Eden. I'll bring up the rear to make sure nothing else goes wrong."

"Now you just wait a minute." The authority in her tone even surprised Eden, but she continued her thoughts anyway, her words gaining speed as she spoke. "You're just going to quit? You're going to let whoever's done this win? I would have thought better of you, Jake Kipling. Now you climb back down, get your bags, and continue sampling. I came to see the mine, and gosh darnit, you're going to show it to me."

Robert laughed as Jake stared at her as if she had two heads. "She's got a point you know. We'll just climb to the next level and start there."

"Fine with me." Jake lowered himself back into the cage, retrieved the equipment, then climbed back out before he bellowed their intentions back to Donald at the surface.

"After you."

Hand, foot, hand, foot. Eden climbed up the cool metal ladder until they reached the next level.

"Stop here, Eden. Robert, you take that adit over there, and we'll sample this one here." Jake pointed to an opening to her right.

"Okay with me." She stepped onto the worn rock floor, Jake right behind her. Then he took her hand and led her into the tunnel. A kaleidoscope of colors met her eyes as the light from her hat danced across the solid walls. Red, gold, white, green, and gray streaked through the rocks.

Eden sucked in a sharp breath as tears filled her eyes.

"What's wrong?"

"It's so beautiful, just like my father told me." Tears of joy and sadness streamed down her face as she reached out and felt the cool rock.

"See? Sometimes it is worth the wait."

Jake turned her to face him, then leaned down and kissed her lightly, not knowing why this one woman had such an effect on him. Why she of all people had managed to steal his heart, where all the others had failed. If he didn't know any better, he'd say he'd fallen in love with her, even though she stood against everything he represented.

And that was why it was suddenly important to share with her what no one else knew. He had to make her understand, and to do that, he had to disclose a family secret. One that had changed the course of his life forever.

Jake moved a shaky hand across the soft skin of Eden's cheek. The time had come, and he realized that a lightness had surrounded him, a sort of peace that he hadn't known he was looking for. This was right. It had to be. "Eden, what's my name?"

"Your name? Jonathan Alexander Kipling. Your friends call you Jake."

"Are you my friend now?"

"I—I—what's your point?" Her hesitation didn't surprise him, nor did her question. This was the Eden he knew. The one who'd captivated his attention since he'd come to town.

"Don't you think it odd I should carry my mother's maiden name?"

"No. You're a Kipling and—what are you trying to tell me, Jake?" She stepped away from him, uncertainty written in her eyes.

But Jake couldn't stop now. He grabbed a deep breath. No one knew except his mother and grandfather and they were both dead now, and he was tired of hiding the truth. "My father's name was Nate Jackson."

Eden's jaw dropped to her chest, which didn't surprise him. The news would shock anyone. Especially in a town as small as Prosperity. How had his parents managed to keep their affair unknown?

"Nate Jackson?" Eden backed further away from him, until her backside was against the rock wall. "Nate Jackson, as in Nate Jackson, Mrs. Jackson's husband?"

"The same."

So that would explain Nana's reaction in the diner

when she saw him that day. But Jake looked nothing like Mr. Jackson. Not really. At least not that she could remember. Jake had blond hair and blue eyes. Mr. Jackson had brown hair and eyes, and judging by the old photographs, was shorter.

Obviously, nobody in town had made the connection either. If Nana had mentioned something, everyone would think she was off her rocker again and remind her to take her medication, because rumor had it that Mr. Jackson was sterile, which was why they'd never had children of their own. Evidently, the problem was with Nana.

"So why are you telling me? And why now? Why didn't you mention something at the town hall meeting?"

Jake stepped forward until he was inches away from her and tilting her head up to gaze into his eyes. "Maybe because I love you." Tenderly, he brushed a wayward strand of hair from her cheek before he leaned down and kissed her again.

His words echoing in her brain, the gentle warmth of his lips as they caressed hers, left her knees weak and her body aching for more as she closed her eyes and wrapped her arms around his neck. "I love you too," she murmured against the corner of his mouth.

The kiss ended sooner than she'd liked, but she realized it was necessary so that neither of them would do something they might regret later. Her thoughts adjusted back to their earlier conversation.

"But Mr. Jackson died along with . . ."

"Which is exactly why I didn't bring it up at the meeting, or the open house. I want people to judge me for what I can accomplish, not because of who my father was."

The only sound in the mine was the muffled tapping of Robert taking samples in the other tunnel, Eden's rapid breathing, and the drip of water somewhere below them.

Eden digested his words carefully. "You're right, Jake. We really aren't that different after all." She leaned forward and gave him a tiny kiss on the cheek. "Now you'd better find me some copper in this mine, or I may just have to do it myself."

Sleep refused to come no matter how many sheep Eden counted. Even the slightly cooler temperatures at night didn't help as she tossed and turned in her bed, so she rose and padded barefoot toward the kitchen. Maybe a warm glass of milk would do the trick. It had always worked before when she couldn't sleep because of the nightmares.

Glass in hand, she headed for the living room and sat in Abuelo's easy chair by the window. Sipping the warm liquid, she looked out at the unpaved street illuminated by the old streetlight on the corner. Nothing stirred in the yellow light.

Her gaze wandered past the street to the mine in the

distance. Mina de Cobre was alive. She'd felt it herself, and seen it on the survey.

Adam was right. Her father did know the risks involved, as well as her grandfather and uncle. Eden had been shielded from it, but deep down, she always knew it existed. Any occupation had its hazards. Accidents occurred driving a car or flying in a plane.

Finishing her milk, she remembered her father's smiling face and gentle strength. Even Eden herself had wanted to work in the mines alongside her family. She was sure that her old miner's hat was hidden somewhere, just waiting for her to reclaim it.

When had the bitterness disappeared?

Jake wasn't her enemy. She was. He'd only been trying to do what was best for the town, she could see that now. She quit denying the truth. Prosperity was in desperate need of jobs and funds to keep going.

She could practically envision Main Street paved, every building restored, an influx of new families instead of old ones leaving. Maybe she and Jake could deepen this love they had for each other. The fact that they had a lot in common, from their love of books to their belief of a better Prosperity, was only the beginning.

Eden set her glass down with a thud. She was in love with Jake Kipling, like she'd told him this afternoon. When had that happened? When had Jake become her knight in shining armor?

The day he'd ridden into town and breathed life

back into it. The same day he'd carried her out of harm's way of that errant baseball. And every day after that when he listened to her tirades and still held her in his arms, comforting her. And even today when he admitted his parentage.

She and Jake were meant for each other. Now all she had to do was convince him of that. And to do that, she had to find out who was responsible for all the vandalism to the mine.

Chapter Eleven

"You've been awful quiet today, honey," Mrs. Jackson said as she took a seat at the counter. "Is something wrong?"

Eden continued to munch on a piece of raisin toast slathered with butter. With her mouth full, she didn't have to answer right away. Besides, how could she say 'I'm in love with Jake, who by the way, is your late husband's illegitimate son?'

Jake. Eden squeezed her eyes shut, trying to block out his image so she could concentrate on an answer. Impossible. His sapphire eyes and the freckles splashed across his face were permanently embedded in her mind. Her love for Jake felt so good as she reached for her cup of coffee and chugged the lukewarm contents.

Then the fear she'd held at bay surfaced. Almost everyone she'd ever loved she'd lost due to the mine. What if she lost Jake too? The cup shattered as it made contact with the counter and a sliver of glass cut her hand. All she could do was stare at the pool of blood forming on her palm.

"Eden Delgado, what on earth is the matter with you?" Mrs. Jackson reached for a paper napkin, picked up her hand, and dabbed at the wound.

"Ouch! I—I—nothing." Avoiding the older woman's eyes, Eden removed the tiny piece of glass embedded in her skin, then busied herself by dumping the rest of the shards into the garbage.

"Sit down, honey, I'll get to that in a minute."

Eden obeyed, still tired from her restless night to argue.

"Now, I've known you too long to know that nothing means something," Mrs. Jackson continued, "but you're stubborn just like your father and your grandfather. So, when you're ready to talk, I'll be here to listen."

Not ready to confide her newfound emotions, or fears, Eden grabbed the older woman's hand and squeezed it gently. "Thanks. You know I'd do the same for you too, Nana." She finished off the rest of her toast and stood. "Let's start cleaning this place up. I've got a lot to do this afternoon."

Clearing the final table together, Eden thought about the pictures she'd found yesterday at the museum of

Mr. Jackson among the rest of the miners. She still didn't see much of a resemblance between Jake and his father, but that didn't mean that Mrs. Jackson didn't recognize him.

Remembering the incident with the ketchup bottle, she looked intently at Mrs. Jackson. Her expression gave away nothing, but all of a sudden, Eden had a sneaking suspicion that she knew—and chose to keep quiet.

She wondered if Mr. Jackson had ever known about his son, or if true to Kipling fashion, the whole incident had been shoved aside. Eden suspected the latter, since no one in town besides Mrs. Jackson had apparently made the connection—yet.

Then another thought struck her. What if Nana was the one responsible for all the vandalism to the mine? She had the potential motive, and Eden had seen her up in the early morning hours that one time, and the next day there'd been an incident. But did she have the knowledge and strength? With or without her medication, Eden doubted it, which left her back at square one.

Her grandfather rounded the corner to grab another cup of coffee and retrieve the bus tub from Eden.

"Abuelo, what happened to your hand?" Eden noticed the two-inch-long scrape on his palm below his index finger.

Her grandfather stared at the cut intensely. "Is nothing. I bang it against the grease trap yesterday." He shrugged, signaling the end of that conversation. Eden didn't question him further, yet the whole thing puzzled her. Abuelo had worked around the trap for decades and to her knowledge had never hurt himself before.

Something wasn't right, but the bell above the door jingled, announcing the arrival of a late customer. A tingling sensation started at her toes and worked its way up to the top of her head. Eden didn't need to turn around to know who stood behind her.

"Hi, Jake."

"Eden. I need to talk to you."

He gently spun her around so she was looking into those crystal blue eyes instead of having to imagine them. Her spirits soared, her heart sang, as she stared at the man she loved. Instinctively, she wanted to push away the worry lines creasing his forehead, massage the tension from his tight shoulders, kiss away the doubts she saw lingering on his lips.

"Likewise, but not here. Let's go to the museum. I have something to show you."

She took his hand and led him to the front door. "I'll be back to settle the books later," she called out to no one in particular as she glanced over her shoulder. Mrs. Jackson gave them a strange look as they exited the restaurant, but it was the haunted expression on Abuelo's face that sent a shiver up and down her spine.

Once inside the old building, Eden grabbed Jake's hand and led him to the stack of photo albums she'd left on the floor. She motioned for him to sit next to her as she plopped down on the floor.

"Now what is it you wanted to talk about?"

His silence surprised her. In fact, Jake hadn't uttered a thing since the restaurant. Eden had never known him to be short on words, but the brackets around his mouth had deepened, and the way he pulled at his ear sent the blood pounding through her veins. The absolute stillness in the museum was getting on her nerves.

"For goodness sake, what's wrong? What happened at the mine this time?"

"How do you know?"

"People talk in this town. I also work in the gossip central of Prosperity. How could I not know?"

Jake passed a tired hand across his face. "Someone's been tampering with the equipment again. Another setback that will cost thousands in lost production. My investors are starting to get worried. If they pull out . . ." He slammed his fist against the floor, raising a tiny puff of dust. So much for her cleaning efforts.

"I thought things had settled down."

"I thought so too."

His sigh spoke volumes, which made her determination to find out whoever was responsible for the vandalism more intense. This had to stop before the damage progressed into violence that could potentially hurt someone. A shudder coursed through her body.

"Was yesterday's problem with the cage due to vandalism or equipment failure?" she questioned softly, praying that it had nothing to do with what was happening at the mine.

"We won't know until it can be looked over in Tucson. Why? Do you know something about it?"

Instead of getting defensive, she took his questioning in stride. Last night had been an awakening for her, a new beginning. One that hopefully included Jake Kipling in her life. "No. I knew nothing yesterday, and I still know nothing today, but that doesn't mean I can't find out."

Eden stared into his eyes and felt peace in the bottomless blue pools. Her mother had always told her that the eyes were the window to a person's soul, and one look into Jake's told her that this lost and tortured man needed her help, whether he knew it or not.

"What exactly does that mean?"

"That's what I wanted to talk to you about," Eden stated simply. "I would have thought after yesterday, you'd realized that I'm not going to fight you on this anymore."

Jake couldn't quite follow her meaning. Weeks of little sleep, and the constant worry over the mine, had eaten away at his ability to think and react quickly. The sincere expression on her face only added to his muddled thoughts.

"You're not going to fight me on what?" he asked tiredly as he tried to rub the sleep from his eyes. Eden was making no sense at all.

"The mine, silly." Her hand gently squeezed his arm as she continued speaking. "I meant every word I said yesterday. I love you, Jonathan Alexander Kipling. While you find me the rest of the copper in the mine, I'll figure out who's responsible for what's been happening to your equipment."

Jake couldn't believe what he was hearing. All these weeks Eden had been opposing him, and suddenly here she was agreeing with him. Her timing couldn't be better.

If she wasn't just giving him a line.

His gaze never strayed from her face. All he could see was the honesty shining from her eyes, the pride etched across the silky smoothness of her cheeks, the passion written on her lips.

His breathing became irregular as he leaned in, her lips mere centimeters from his own. The beat of his heart drowned out the soft growl from his throat. Her eyes closed in anticipation, but he knew now was not the time for such intimacies. Not when his life was still in limbo, not until he knew who he really was.

Yesterday he thought he knew. Today he wasn't so sure.

As he fell back against the wall in defeat, he ran an unsteady hand through his hair. This woman, who had the power to make his life complete, also had the power to make his life a living hell.

"Jake Kipling, what's bothering you?"

He sighed in frustration. Eden knew who she was,

knew where she was going, and from where she came. Half of the things Jake had no idea about. He hoped Eden had some of his answers here. "I don't know who I am anymore."

Eden remained silent. Jake, who was always so confident and sure, was questioning himself. Hesitantly, she wrapped her arms around his middle.

"You remember what you told me on the way to Tucson, Jake? What counts is what's in your head and heart. You are who you are, Jake. You're not really a Kipling or a Jackson. You're a combination of the two. Nate Jackson was a wonderful man—as I'm sure your mother was an exceptional woman. We have to quit letting the past dictate our future."

"But the past is who we are."

"Not if you don't want it to be. You can't change the past, Jake, but you can change the future. You can make it anything you want it to be."

Eden rested her head on Jake's shoulder. It felt so right, so comfortable. The feeling washed over her that this was where she was meant to be. "If you're ready, I found some pictures of your father. We can look at them if you'd like. Maybe they'll answer some of your questions."

Together, until the afternoon sun set over the western mountains, Jake and Eden pored through the old mining albums stacked in the corner of the museum.

"Mrs. Jackson, come in. What can I do for you today?" Jake was surprised by the unexpected visit, though he should have suspected something especially after the long look the woman had given him yesterday at the diner.

"I think you know why I'm here." The matronly woman heaved her body into the oversized chair by the desk. Once seated, she patted a stray hair back in place and clutched at her purse. The white knuckles contrasted with the brown leather, and Jake realized she wasn't as calm and composed as she led him to believe.

"How long have you known?" Steepling his fingers against his mouth, Jake regarded her compassionately. Nothing had been easy since he'd come here, but aside from Eden, meeting this woman, the one who'd had an influence on his father's life, like his mother, was hard—on both of them.

"I suspected from the beginning. I knew my Nate well."

Leaning back in his chair, Jake broke his hands apart and tugged at his earlobe, unable to stop himself. Maybe he should put the stupid earring back in and be done with it. Then at least he'd have a reason. "Why did you wait till now to see me?"

"Well . . ." Lines of strain bracketed her mouth, but they softened as soon as she attempted to smile. "Eden's not the only one who needs to put the past to rest. My Nate—your father—well, stop over at my place sometime, I'll tell you all about him."

As she stood to leave, Jake stopped her. "Mrs. Jackson, wait. Why haven't you told anyone in town?"

"Oh, no one would believe me. Most people in Prosperity think I'm crazy anyway. I did tell Julio, Eden's grandfather, but it took a lot to convince him. I figure when you're good and ready you'll admit the truth." Her gaze leveled on him. "Have you told anyone?"

"Just Eden."

The widow sank back in the chair.

"Well, that certainly would explain her unusual actions today."

"Are you okay, Mrs. Jackson?"

"I must admit that after all these years, it's a relief to know the truth. I always knew I wasn't the love of Nate's life, though he would never tell me so. I could sense it in the way he held me and touched me."

"I'm sure that's not true, Mrs. Jackson."

"Oh, he loved me in his own way, but not with that undying love you read about all the time."

Like how Jake felt about Eden.

"Now I can understand his words and actions." She dabbed at her eyes with a piece of tissue she'd pulled from her purse. "Nate would have been so proud to have a son. I couldn't give him one, you know. But Mary could. Well, I'd better get back to the diner. Julio is waiting from me."

"Are you sure you're okay with this?" Jake couldn't believe she was taking this all so well. Or was she? Almost out of habit, he glanced at her hands, noticing the well-worn hands of age, and a cut or two. He shook his head. What he was thinking was impossible.

"Of course I'm okay. We mining breed are one tough stock." He didn't doubt that for a second as she rose from her seat and shuffled to the door before turning back to face him. "There is one other thing. Eden is like a daughter to me. If you do anything to hurt her, anything at all, you're going to have to answer to both Julio and me. Is that clear?"

The door shut with a resounding thud as Jake stared at the space Mrs. Jackson had just occupied. "Yes, ma'am." But the words died on his lips as he saw her mount Eden's bicycle with ease and ride away.

The sound of tires rolling over loose gravel woke Eden from a light sleep. For a moment, she lay there trying to identify the sound until it registered in her brain it was a car. And not just any car. Abuelo's Chevy. Cautiously, she peered out her window in time to see her grandfather throw something in the back seat, then settle himself in the front and carefully back out of the alley. Where was he going?

An uneasy feeling crossed over her. She ran to the front of the apartment and looked out of the window just in time to see her grandfather turn onto Main.

Instead of preparing for the breakfast crowd, at four–thirty in the morning, Abuelo was going to the mine.

So he'd been the one behind all the disturbances. Eden should've seen the signs. His tiredness, the unexplained cuts and bruises on his hands. She'd been looking outside, when she should have been looking within. She was so naive. She had to stop him.

Eden dashed back to her room and threw on the clothes she'd worn earlier. In a flash she was downstairs and out the door. Now what? Abuelo had taken their only vehicle. She'd never make it to the mine in time to stop him on her bike, much less on foot. Adam's car was in the shop and Mrs. Jackson didn't own one. Calling Tyler was out of the question—she didn't want to involve the sheriff's deputy.

Eden spied old Mr. Davis's motor scooter parked across the street at the Dry Gulch Restaurant & Bar. Great, he must have tied one over again. She ran to the dilapidated vehicle, saying a silent prayer of thanks that the keys hung so innocently from the ignition. If she didn't run out of gas, she'd have the scooter back before anyone noticed it missing. She hopped on, turned the switch, and rode after her grandfather.

"Why, Abuelo? Why?" She followed him as fast as the motor scooter would carry her. Which wasn't very fast at all. "Darn this thing," she cried out in frustration, realizing she'd never make it to the mine to stop her grandfather from doing whatever it was he planned.

Chapter Twelve

"Put it down, Eden."

Eden squinted, trying to stare past the flashlight's glare before she dropped the hose and shielded her eyes from the light. Jake. The shattered look on his face made the lump in her throat ache. She swallowed but the lump was still there.

"Jake, I can—I'm sorry. I was—" She was what? Busted. Red-handed. There was no way she could explain her way out of this without mentioning her grandfather. Not when the evidence lay between them.

"You were, what," he stated matter-of-factly, "fixing my equipment again? Like the other times?"

A coyote howled in the distance, its mournful cry echoing around them. She stared at the ground, unable to look him in the eye, longing to tell him that she wasn't responsible. That she was only trying to help him.

But if she told him that, then she'd have to tell him who was responsible. Images of Abuelo flashed through her mind. How he'd always been there for her when she hurt herself. How he'd listen attentively to her stories and dreams. How he'd kept the family together when their world was crumbling apart.

Then she thought about Adam, Lori, her niece and nephew, the rest of the town, and the influence Abuelo maintained as a steadfast member of Prosperity. No. If it was Eden they wouldn't be surprised, but her grandfather was too old, too well-liked, to have this matter come to light in the remaining years of his life.

Her gaze traveled back to Jake's face as he aimed the light back to the front loader she'd been trying to fix. Even in the dimness, the lines of fatigue and strain were apparent, as were the signs of defeat. His stooped shoulders and grim smile attested to that.

She longed to reach out and touch him, to ease his pain. The mine was still between them, just not in the way she'd expected. And that was the price she had to pay. Eden loved Jake, but she also loved her family.

Her throat constricted as she watched him thrust his hand through his already disheveled hair. There was nothing she could do or say that would make any of this disappear. Her decision was made.

"So yesterday was all a lie." His hoarse voice broke the unsteady silence. "Everything you said at the museum was to throw me off guard. What else did you have planned?" He grabbed her upper arms and shook her gently. "What else is going to go wrong?"

Eden's eyes misted over. As before, her world was shattering around her and there was nothing she could do about it.

"I'm sorry, Jake."

"I'm sorry too, Eden."

Jake swept her into his arms as his lips claimed hers. Why of all the women in the world did he have to fall in love with the one who stood between him and his dreams? Why did her touch, her laughter, her passion, make him whole and bring light into the dark areas of his life? Because his love for her matched the love his father had for his mother until Charles Kipling broke it apart.

As their embrace deepened, the shame of his parentage disappeared, made possible by the one woman he couldn't have. He stilled, and lifted his head, just in time to hear the sound of footsteps approaching.

"Looks like we found our vandal, Mr. Kipling." Delbert Cummings, the night watchman, stated as he flashed his light across the surface of the equipment, then Eden. "Like father like daughter, I see."

Eden stood rigid in Jake's arms. She'd never liked Mr. Cummings, though she didn't know why. Maybe it was his weak chin and lazy attitude, and the fact that he never managed to meet her gaze every time their paths crossed.

"What's that supposed to mean?" Jake questioned softly, his grip tightening on her waist. Eden leaned into him, accepting his protectiveness and strength.

Delbert Cummings paused, an uncertain expression crossing his features as if he suddenly realized he'd spoken out of turn. "Well—um—ah—"

Jake took a step forward, dragging Eden with him. One gaze at the murderous expression on his face only confirmed that he was not a force to be reckoned with. "Answer me, Cummings. What do you know about the accident and the vandalism going on here?"

As if realizing the game was up, the slightly overweight man's words came out in a rush. "Uh—your family wasn't responsible for the accident, Mr. Kipling. Eden's was."

"No! You're lying." Eden would have collapsed if Jake hadn't been holding her. "I don't believe you."

"Then why is your grandfather trying to keep the mine shut if it's not the truth?"

Eden had no response and felt herself begin to tremble. The night watchman's words made sense. Why would Abuelo be vandalizing the mine if there was nothing to hide?

But her father? How had Eden not known the truth? Blackness descended over her that had nothing to do with the still, dark night. Her world was crumbling apart as she struggled to remain standing. Her father, the man she'd loved and worshipped, was a murderer, pure and simple.

All these years, she'd blamed an innocent family. The Kiplings weren't to blame. The Delgados were.

Her whole life had been a lie.

Having heard enough, she wiggled out of Jake's embrace and disappeared into the night.

"I think this belongs to you?" Jake held out an old battered baseball cap as he trapped Eden's grandfather by the griddle, preparing to cook the bacon for the morning.

The old man turned slowly to face him. "Where'd you find that?" He questioned in a gruff voice.

"At the mine where you dropped it, where else?"

"I dunno what you're talking about."

But Jake stopped him before he could pivot back to the griddle by placing a hand on his arm. "Then you're going to let Eden take the blame for everything that's happened?"

"I still dunno what you're talking about. I have food to make—"

"The game's up, Mr. Delgado. We caught Eden at the mine tonight with the front loader wires in her hand. Your baseball hat was underneath it. Now, unless you start talking, Eden will be heading to the nearest jail at daybreak because she's decided to protect you."

A lie, since they'd let her go, but Delgado didn't need to know that unless Eden had already confronted her grandfather. Somehow he doubted that because

Delgado looked at him in surprise. Eden's loyalty to her family stung at his insides, but he couldn't fault her for it. He'd do the same thing in her place, which left him with a sense of loss because he'd wanted that all for himself.

Her grandfather's face crumbled before his eyes. He didn't answer right away; instead he reached out and turned the griddle off, shuffled out of the kitchen to the coffee machine where he poured them both a cup of coffee, then motioned him to sit at the counter beside him.

"You're a smart boy, like your father."

"I'll take that as a compliment."

Silence lingered as Eden's grandfather stared at the black contents in his cup, his expression grim, his skin tone pale against the early morning light. When Julio Delgado rubbed a hand across his eyes, Jake realized then that he was crying.

Tension, mixed with apprehension twisted his gut. If what had happened had reduced this brave, strong man to tears, he could only imagine what it was doing to Eden. After he finished here, he had to go to her, tell her he still loved her, and that nothing mattered anymore except her happiness, even if it meant the end of the mining tradition for his family. But first, he needed answers.

"Eden knows the truth now that the cave-in was planned. Do you know why?"

Delgado spoke in Spanish under his breath and Jake

couldn't understand him, but he let the old man's mind wander for a moment. He wasn't going anywhere any time soon. Still, he wasn't ready when the words finally came.

"Eden's father wasn't alone." Eyes still bright with moisture, Delgado gave him a sympathetic look that did little to prepare him for the reality of his next sentence. "Your father, along with many others, caused the accident that killed everyone that day."

Jake felt the blood drain from his face as the old man's words sank in. Nate Jackson was also responsible? His voice cracked. "What? Why?"

"The men were bought off by the Henderson Mine to shut down Mina de Cobra. They planned on dynamiting the tunnels when everyone was out, but something went wrong."

"You can say that again." Jake thought he was going to get sick.

"It was to look like an accident." Delgado took another large sip of coffee, the expression on his face still grim. "It's not too hard when you know what to do. I never figure out why your father did it, but now I know it was to get back at Charles Kipling."

"So by vandalizing the mine, you hoped to deter me, make me go home, because I might have discovered something the investigators missed." Dawning comprehension settled across his shoulders. "You also took the surveys that disappeared at the museum, didn't you? Where are they?"

"*Si*. I knew if you saw them, you'd see the numbers had been changed. I destroyed them."

"In order to protect us," Jake stated simply.

"To protect myself." Delgado's fist crashed down on the counter, upsetting both cups of coffee. Suddenly his hand latched onto Jake's arm, pinning him to his seat. "Is bad enough Eden knows her father did it. If she find out that I, Julio Delgado, did nothing to stop it, it will destroy her. I won't let that happen."

Freeing himself from Delgado's grip, Jake understood the meaning of his words. "Eden is stronger and smarter than you realize, Mr. Delgado. She knows you were behind all the vandalism. It won't take her long to figure out why. I've got to see her. Excuse me."

As Jake got up to leave, Delgado stopped him again. "Wait. There's more." The sound of the stool scraping on the worn linoleum floor, along with the urgency in the old man's voice, sent a chill through him. So did the clomping of several pairs of feet on the wooden steps out back.

Adam, Tyler, and Mrs. Jackson rushed through the service door, Lucky not too far behind.

"Where's Eden?" Adam demanded, his disheveled appearance suggested he'd been woken from a deep sleep. "What's all this nonsense she was talking about concerning our father and the mine this morning?"

"I hope she's upstairs," Jake answered to Adam's retreating back.

A minute later, Adam returned, a wild look in his eyes. "Her bed's empty. She's not here."

"She's not here?" Mrs. Jackson's concerned voice cracked. The older woman collapsed onto the stool next to Eden's grandfather. "Julio, where could she be?"

Apprehension coursed through Jake's body. It didn't seem like Eden to just take off like that. From the distraught looks of her family, it wasn't something she'd ever done. Surely she didn't think he'd do anything to her grandfather.

Jake broke into a sweat as an uneasy silence shrouded the room. "The mine," Jake spoke, breaking the heavy atmosphere. That's the only place she could be."

"No, *Dios*, No." Delgado's face turned ashen as he gasped for air. He spoke in bits and pieces of broken English and Spanish.

"What's he saying?" Jake stopped pacing the room and advanced upon the old man until Tyler stepped in, thrusting a hand out to stop him.

"He has set dynamite charges to go off and seal the mine for good. No one was supposed to be there this morning. Let's go."

Adam yanked the door open as the deputy sheriff grabbed Jake around the arm and pulled him out of the diner. Good thing too, or he might have done something to Eden's grandfather in his anger over Delgado's final action.

* * *

Eden could run away from Jake and the episode at the mine last night, but she couldn't run from the truth. For the last hour she'd thought about nothing except Delbert Cummings's words. Guilt wrenched her heart and soul, and nothing would bring her peace until she righted the wrongs. As a Delgado, she would turn herself in and insist that Jake press charges.

The Kiplings had always wanted what was best for the town. Even Jake. It was her family that had ruined everything because of greed.

She knew what she had to do now.

After she apologized to Jake, she intended to go to the local sheriff's substation and demand that Tyler, or whoever was on duty, arrest her. Which was why she was on her way back to the mine. The mansion had been empty, and so had the surveyor's office, which meant Mina de Cobra was the only place left for him to go.

"Jake?" Eden could barely shout; her lungs hurt from the exertion of running. "Jake, where are you?" She jiggled the handle; the office was locked. Maybe he was working on the equipment? No one. Though the hoses appeared to have been put back in place.

But where else could he be? The mine. Eden swallowed nervously. Surely Jake wouldn't go in there alone? No one went in by themselves because of the risk and danger involved. Her heart began to beat furiously in her chest. With Robert back in New York for a few days on business, surely Jake wouldn't—before she could take another step, Eden tumbled to the ground from the blast of hot air emanating from the entrance to the mine.

Images of the first explosion paraded through her memory. She screamed in terror as she covered her ears, trying to block out the noise. This was not happening again. But as she sat there, the deafening roar of tumbling rocks echoed in her ears as a layer of dust hovered overhead.

Protected from rocks and timber by the front loader, she was surrounded by the settling dirt. The fine coating covered her hair, skin, and clothes, and she coughed as the grit and dust irritated her throat.

Then the noise stopped, leaving an eerie silence in its wake.

"Jake?" Eden crawled to where the entrance used to be. Rocks and debris blocked her path. Just like before. Eden clawed at the largest boulder, using the weight of her body to try and dislodge it. Nothing. She only managed to bruise her shoulder and remove the skin from the pads of her fingers. This time there were no sirens, no way to notify the town of the disaster. She was on her own. She had no time to try and get to town for help while Jake was somewhere in the mine.

"Jake?" she whimpered as she slid down the face of the rock. Exhaustion strained her muscles, but she didn't give up. She wouldn't fail Jake. Not now. Not when her heart told here he was still alive and needed her.

Flinging back the hair that had fallen into her eyes, she renewed her efforts by starting with the smaller stones. Ones she could easily move aside. If she could clear the boulder, she might just be able to use leverage to move it, or hot-wire the front loader to get it out of the way.

She would not lose another loved one to the mine.

Methodically, she threw the small boulders to her left and began to clear a small section. Dirt burned her eyes and made breathing difficult, but she didn't care as she wiped her forehead with the back of her hand. Jake's sapphire blue eyes haunted her; his smile teased and tempted her. His voice mesmerized her.

As the sun inched its way over Sumner's Peak, Eden could swear she heard him calling out to her. But she couldn't tell where the voice had come from the dust hovering in the air distorted everything. She renewed her struggle with the larger boulders as she continued to try and clear the entrance.

"Eden." Jake's voice sounded closer now, and not from beneath the boulders, but from her right.

Confusion mingled with the terror still trapped in her heart, but her hands fell away from the jagged rock she was attempting to dislodge. If Jake wasn't in the mine, then he was okay. She swatted at the layer of dust, trying to clear her vision as a dark shadow emerged.

"Jake." Flinging her arms around his neck, she welcomed his strength as his own arms wrapped protectively around her middle. Tears that refused to fall earlier coursed down her dirt-stained cheeks.

"Woman, you just gave me the biggest scare of my life." Jake's knuckles gently grazed her cheek as his other hand caressed her back. "What are you doing here?"

"I—I—"

"Did you find her?" Tyler's voice cut her off.

"Is she okay?" Adam questioned, stepping in behind the deputy sheriff.

Eden's gaze flew to where her brother and Tyler had materialized in the early morning light. The concern, then relief etched on their faces matched Jake's.

"She's fine." Jake held her closer. "Can we have a few minutes please?"

A look of understanding crossed his features as Tyler stepped back, his hand on Adam's shoulder. "Sure. No problem. We'll be by the car when you're ready."

As the sound of their footsteps ceased, Eden rested her head against the solid wall of Jake's chest; the steady beat of his heart gave her energy to continue. "Jake. I'm sorry. I came to apologize for all the trouble, then turn myself in."

"What?" His fingers cupped her chin and lifted her head so that she had no choice but to look at him. His sapphire blue eyes brimmed with a tenderness, a passion, that left her breathless. "Turn yourself in for what?"

"For this." Her response was barely above a whisper as she broke her gaze and surveyed the damage around her. Nothing remained of the opening to the mine. All of Jake's hard work over the past few weeks had been reduced to a pile of rocks and dirt.

"Eden. There's no reason to apologize or turn yourself in for something you didn't do."

"But—"

"Shhh." He silenced her by placing a finger over her lips. "I won't let you take the blame for your grandfather's actions any more than I can let you take the blame for your father's."

"Why?"

"Because your father wasn't the only one involved all those years ago. My father was just as guilty as the rest of them."

"Nate Jackson too? Who told you?"

"Your grandfather."

Resting her head against his chest again, she absorbed his strength as her arms wrapped tighter around his neck. "Oh, Jake. I'm so sorry. You must feel terrible."

"Not as bad as your grandfather feels. He was only doing what he thought was best."

A wave of sadness crashed through her. The knowledge that her grandfather knew what had happened twenty years ago and remained silent had to have been a heavy burden. "So what will happen to Abuelo?"

"I don't know. Unfortunately, he and Delbert Cummings will have to take responsibility for their actions. There's no way around it, but I'll see what I can do."

"Delbert Cummings?"

"Who do you think was paying our fathers off all those years ago when he was working for the Henderson Mine? He was also helping your grandfather with the vandalism because he didn't want the truth to come out either."

More sorrow touched her soul as she realized Jake spoke the truth. Abuelo had meant well, but his actions could have caused someone else to get hurt, and that was not something Eden could take lightly. "What about the mine?"

A momentary flash of disappointment straightened his shoulders before he planted a light kiss on her forehead. "It doesn't matter anymore. I love you, Eden. Nothing is more important than you are. Not my money, not my pride, and certainly not the mine."

"What?" She shrugged out of his arms and took a step back, almost tripping over a rock. Jake steadied her before she did such an ungraceful thing as falling. "You're going to quit just like that?" Her arms crossed over her chest, she gave him a piercing look. "I don't believe you, Jake Kipling. After all we've been through together—wait a minute—did you just say you still loved me?"

"Yes. I'd shout it from the top of Sumner's Peak if I thought Charles could hear me. I never stopped loving you, even when it looked like everything was falling apart."

"Oh, Jake. I love you too." Jake was truly her knight in shining armor. She threw her arms back around his neck determined that nothing would ever stand in their way again. "But that doesn't mean I'm going to let you give up. The town needs you. I need you. I didn't lose you to the mine; the mine brought us together. Don't you see?"

The love and admiration shining from Jake's eyes was more than she could bear. Eden lifted her lips, readying herself for his tender caress as the dust continued to settle around them.

She didn't have to wait long.

In the distance, she heard the sounds of the town waking up along with the creatures of the day. Prosperity belonged to the mine. And the mine belonged to Prosperity.

Neither Eden nor Jake was responsible for what had happened in the past, only the present and the future. A future working together, as their ancestors did before them.